The Adventures of Surf Dude:
The Dog of Ochlockonee Bay

The Adventures of
Surf Dude:
The Dog of Ochlockonee Bay

Zelle Andrews

turtle dove press
Tallahassee, Florida

Paperback ISBN: 978-1-947536-09-8

Ebook ISBN: 978-1-947536-10-4

Library of Congress Control Number: 2021937728

Printed in the United States of America

The text of this book was typeset in Palatino Linotype.

Cover design by Elizabeth Babski

Front cover photo of Surf Dude © Mary Andrews

Back cover photos of Surf Dude and the water tower © M.R. Street

With your purchase of this book, you are supporting dog rescue groups. Thank you!

10 9 8 7 6 5 4 3 2 1   1 2 3 4 5 6 7 8 9 10

I dedicate this book to all the stray dogs
searching for their 'forever homes'
and the tender-hearted people who care for them.
Thank you.

Chapter One

I didn't mean to be famous. I'm just your average yellow dog that once was loved, but became a drifter unexpectedly. I'm not sure what I'm looking for, perhaps a place where thunder, shotguns, fireworks, and mean people with cowboy boots don't exist.

My story began in the deep woods of South Carolina. I was born in an abandoned fox den with six other puppies. My first taste of life was where the longleaf pines touched the belly of the clouds, cypress roots disappeared in dark waters, and pinecones fell from the trees to become chew toys. It was rare to see a human in this part of the cypress swamps. That's why Mama preferred to hunt here; we were safe from people and she could teach us her methods of stalking and pouncing on prey. It was mostly just a game for us, though, and we entertained ourselves by stalking and pouncing on each other.

My last memory of my brothers and sisters was watching them play near a shallow creek, splashing along the banks and pouncing on tadpoles. For once, instead of joining in, I watched Mama stalk a rabbit. I scrutinized the manner in which she moved, her body lowered in the tall grass, her tail curved over her back, and her ears perked high. She didn't move a muscle except for her amber eyes, following the rabbit as it hopped about merrily, blind to the fact it was going to be our evening meal. Rabbit, squirrel, and fresh creek water, nothing tasted better.

1

Mama inched closer to the rabbit, through the tall grass, while it nibbled on tender shoots. She was a few feet away when the wind changed direction for a brief second and then it hit me full force in the face: The smell of fear. The rabbit's fear. It knew a predator was nearby.

Mama pounced but missed the frightened rabbit. The chase was on. The rabbit disappeared in the grass, Mama close behind. The swaying of the grass tops was the only indication of which direction she chased the rabbit. My brothers, sisters, and I focused on Mama, quivering with anticipation of our meal. We were so intent on Mama and the rabbit that we didn't hear someone approaching behind us until it was too late. What I thought was a cloud overhead blocking out the sun, was the man's shadow, hovering over us.

My siblings scattered in different directions, but I was cornered between jutting roots and large rocks in the embankment. He snatched me by the nape of my neck and stuffed me in his oversized camo coat before Mama realized what happened.

My brothers and sisters howled in alarm when I was thrown in the back of his truck. I landed hard on my shoulder on the truck-bed. I scrambled to my feet and put my paws on the side of the truck to search for Mama. I saw her running for me, but the truck took off and dust swallowed her. That was the last time I ever saw Mama or my brothers and sisters.

I was too small to jump out of the truck and bounced around with every turn on the uneven gravel road. By the time we got to where he was going, I was pretty riled up.

I growled like I'd seen Mama do at the animals that bothered us. It didn't scare him one bit. He spat brown liquid and grabbed the nape of my neck again. I hated when he did that. Even Mama didn't do that anymore. I was too big for it.

He carried me into a house and took me in a back room. "Here," he said, dropping me down in a woman's lap, "Happy birthday."

She squealed a high-pitch sound like the animals do when Mama catches them. "Oh, Leo, she's adorable."

Leo stood over us. "It's a boy, not a girl. I got the first one I could grab."

She smiled at him. "Thank you."

I was too frightened to move. I'd never been this close to a human before, and I certainly had never been touched by one. At night when out hunting with Mama, we often watched people from the edge of the woods at the campgrounds, but we always waited until after dark when everyone was asleep before stealing food that had fallen, unnoticed, under the picnic tables. Mama taught us to never trust humans.

I wiggled and squirmed, trying to escape, but the woman held tight. Her long fingernails scratched a spot under my neck that had been bothering me for a few days. I tried to help by scratching it too with my back foot, but I was only kicking air.

"I love him," she beamed.

"He'll be an outside dawg, Jorene," the man barked from the other room. "I won't have that dawg taking up my space in the bed or couch." A door slammed.

Jorene rubbed behind my ears. That felt good too. She leaned over, rubbed her face in my fur, and scrunched up her nose. "You're a stinky little fella."

Next thing I knew, she dunked me neck-deep in warm water and massaged weird smelly stuff in my fur. She didn't even mind that I tinkled in the water a bit.

"You're going to smell so much better. I'll be right back with a towel." I played in the warm water until she returned. I fought harder than I'd ever fought with my brothers and sisters trying to get the towel away from her. She always managed to get it away from me, though. My brothers and sisters would have loved this game.

Leo stood in the doorway with a disapproving look. "You better scrub that tub tonight." He sniffed, scrunched his nose, and disappeared.

I snatched the towel from Jorene with my teeth and started ripping it when the water made a sucking sound. Curious, I placed my paws on the edge of the white wall and looked at the water. It was disappearing down a hole. How'd she make it do that? I'd never seen the creek in the woods do that.

Leo left and Jorene pulled me up on the bed with her. Later that night, just as I drifted off to sleep beside her, she slipped something over my head and around my neck. It reminded me of the wild vines in the woods which frequently got tangled around my legs. Mama always rescued me. I had to get this vine off before it strangled me. My back foot was almost underneath it when I lost my balance and fell over. Jorene touched me gently.

"No, no. Don't do that," she said, adjusting the vine tighter. "This was Sasha's collar before she died. She was a Catahoula. It's a little big, but I'm sure you'll grow into it. I'm sorry I can't adjust it any smaller."

I didn't like it, not one bit. I never saw Mama or my brothers and sisters wear something like this.

"Let's go potty. Leo wouldn't like it if you had an accident."

As if the collar wasn't bad enough, she tied something long to it that looked even more like a vine, and pulled me outside. It was torture. I twisted, rolled on my back, wrestled with the vine, and tried to run away. I even tried to gnaw it off, but I couldn't break free. In a last-ditch effort, I threw my head back and bayed louder than I'd ever bayed before, hoping Mama would hear me.

"Calm down, little fella," Jorene said. "You'll get used to your collar and leash." I ran circles around her trying to break free. Finally, I collapsed beside her, panting with exhaustion. As irritated as I was, when she scratched me behind my ear, I leaned into it and closed my eyes. She was tricky, this one.

Leo bellowed from the house and Jorene stiffened.

"You know, one day I'm going to be brave enough to leave him, and you're coming with me," Jorene whispered. "I always told Sasha that we'd do that, but…"

Her gentle voice calmed me and she continued to talk about Sasha, Leo, and leaving. The vine slipped carelessly between my two front paws. While she was lost in conversation, I chewed and planned my escape.

"Sasha was like a girlfriend that I could tell anything to. I asked Leo to find me another girl dog, but you'll do. I'm sure we'll be great friends."

Loud banging sounds came from the house. "Jorene, where's my chewing tobacco?"

She sighed. "He's not always like this. Sometimes he's real nice. He's just been stressed since I've been sick and lost my job." She stood up, pulled the vine, and it snapped. Faster than Mama catching a rabbit, she snatched me up.

"I can't believe you chewed through Sasha's leash. Tricky little boy," she scolded. Her smile told me she wasn't really mad.

That night on the back porch, I tried to get settled in the large cardboard box stuffed with old towels. Thoughts of Mama and my brothers and sisters filled my head. Were they missing me as much as I missed them? The towels kept me warm, but they had each other. I wanted to go home. I raised my nose and called to them.

Jorene stepped out on the porch, pressed a finger to her lips, and laid flat on the concrete facing me. "Shh, don't wake Leo." She slipped a piece of something gooey to me.

I'd never tasted anything like it, except when I chewed a pinecone with sap on it.

"I love honey buns. It's one of my weaknesses."

I licked all the gooey stuff from between her fingers, and she kissed my nose. I don't know what got into me, but I licked gooey stuff from her face too.

"So, I guess your name is Honeybun." She scratched me behind my ear. "Sleep tight, sweet Honeybun." Jorene slipped back inside. I wasn't sure about my new home, but I knew one thing: Honey buns sure beat sappy pinecones.

Chapter Two

Jorene often slipped me in the house when Leo wasn't home. He griped about the dog hair, but then ignored us. I'd grown fond of Jorene, but didn't trust Leo. He was loud, mean, and stomped around in pointy-toed shoes he called cowboy boots. He never would have agreed to let me stay in the house at night if not for the rat.

It was half-way in Leo's bag of chewing tobacco when I found it. I pounced, missed, and chased it around the bedroom, knocking over a small lamp and a potted plant, until I cornered it in the bathroom. It was over before Leo and Jorene had a chance to run into the bedroom to check out the commotion. I thought Leo would yell at me about the mess, but once he saw his bag of chewing tobacco with markings of rat teeth on it, he nodded.

"I knew I picked a good one." That's the only time he ever said anything nice about me.

I never did see another rat in the house, but I always stayed alert, just in case.

After I caught the rat, Leo agreed to let me in the house, but I wasn't allowed on the bed, at least not when he was there. Jorene and I worked well as a team. I would snuggle with her on the bed until I heard the rumble of his truck outside. When I jumped down, she flipped the covers over to hide the dog hair.

I loved snuggling with Jorene and sharing her honey buns. She was the only one I trusted. Only once was I not happy with

Jorene. She took me to see this man who pinched my hind leg and I fell asleep. I woke up with some sort of bucket strapped around my head and an ache near where I go potty. Leo yelled each time I bumped the walls and furniture during the night, but I couldn't help it. That bucket was the problem.

Jorene was much nicer. "It was your idea to get him neutered. We only have to deal with the cone for a few more days." So that's what they put on my head, a cone. I never thought anything would be worse than a collar and leash until I met the cone.

◊◊◊

Jorene coughed more frequently and often stayed in bed all day. She wasn't able to find a job either, and Leo yelled that she wasn't trying hard enough. The yelling seemed to make her cough even more.

The day Jorene shooed me off the bed and onto the couch, so she could sleep more comfortably, was a bad day for us. Leo's truck rumbled up in the driveway and I sprang from the couch. I tried to wake Jorene to clean my dog hairs off the couch, but she brushed me away.

Leo stomped in, grabbed a beer, and sat on the couch.

I did something I'd never done before; I sat at Leo's feet and whined, pawing at his cowboy boots. He needed to check on Jorene.

"Jorene, come get this dog!" Leo yelled, taking a long gulp of his beer. "He's shedding all over my clothes and I'm going out with the guys tonight."

Jorene shuffled into the kitchen, popped a bag of popcorn, and crawled back in the bed.

"Honeybun, come here," she called. I never ignored her, especially if it involved a chance to eat popcorn.

She turned on the big box of moving pictures and patted the covers beside her. "Come watch TV with me."

I hesitated for a moment because Leo was there, but then I jumped up and immediately snuggled against the warmth of her thigh, resting my face inches from the bowl of popcorn. One piece fell from her hand and I scooped it up quickly. I don't know if she did it on purpose or by accident, but it was all mine. She slipped me another piece.

"This is my favorite part of the movie," she whispered, not taking her eyes off the moving pictures. "Here, right here," she pointed at the TV. "This is where he tells her he can't live without her and will love her forever." Leo grumbled from the living room and I snuggled closer. "Some girls are so lucky," she sighed, throwing a piece of popcorn at the door.

"Jorene, where are my keys?" Leo hollered. "The guys are waiting for me."

"They're in here, by the television."

Cowboy boots clomped on the floor and Leo stormed into the bedroom. Jorene and I both hated those boots, but for different reasons: I hated them because they hurt when they landed on my back side. She hated the sound of them because she knew he was heading out to drink and when he came home, he'd yell and throw things.

Leo grabbed his keys. "You couldn't have gotten up and brought them to me?" He scowled at the TV, rolling his eyes. "You know that ain't real life, right? He ain't gonna make her happy and she sure ain't gonna make him happy." He pulled her wallet out of her purse.

"What are you doing?" she asked.

"I need money for the poker game tonight." He stuffed crinkly paper in his jeans pocket.

"I need that for my medicine I'm picking up tomorrow morning. I'm almost out." Her hand tightened on my fur. I hoped she wouldn't get upset; she coughed more when she was upset.

"It ain't helping you anyway." He glared at me then walked to the kitchen. I heard the clink of his beer bottles.

"That's because you won't take me to get reevaluated to adjust the dosage. Dr. Hamilton said I'm three months past my yearly exam. He won't prescribe anymore unless I go in."

"So go," he barked.

Jorene shifted in the bed. I crawled up on her legs to comfort her. "You know I can't drive. I need you to take me." Her voice faded, either from being tired or from trying to soothe his anger. If she hoped it would make him be nice, it didn't work. It never worked.

"Take the bus."

"They don't have busses down here, Leo, you know that."

He stormed back in the room. "Figure it out, and get that mutt off the bed." He scowled at me. "I'm tired of itching at night with all the dirt he leaves on the sheets!"

I lowered my ears. I knew getting on the bed when Leo was home was a bad idea.

"Hop down, Honeybun." Jorene patted my rear. I obeyed, but didn't take my eyes off those cowboy boots for one minute. Leo was fast, but most of the time, I was faster; most of the time.

"Leo, please don't take all the money. I can get Pat next door to take me tomorrow, but I need money to get my meds."

I hoped Leo would just leave and not come back that night. Sometimes he stayed away for three or four days, and Jorene and I snuggled all day long. She'd feed me popcorn, chunks of cheese, honey buns, and lots of other stuff. She tried dog food several times, but I never cared for it.

"I do a lot for you, Jorene. Like when you wanted this dawg a few months ago. I even paid to get him neutered so he'd settle down some."

They'd argued the week before, too, when he took "beer money" out of her purse.

"I only get the checks once a month and it barely covers the cost of my meds."

"Don't give me crap about this." He stepped closer to her.

Leo is predictable. I knew what was coming: Boots kicking and hands hitting. I didn't mean to do it, I'd never done it before, but when Leo advanced on Jorene, I growled at him.

"You better control your dawg, or I will."

My eyes went to his cowboy boots. I stood almost in the corner of the room, between the bed and window. If he kicked, I didn't have much room to avoid it.

"Shush, Honeybun," Jorene said.

"Honeybun, that's the most stupidest name I ever heard of. You should have let me name him."

Jorene despised it when he talked about me. She took a lot from him, but not when it came to me.

"Just go, take the money," she snapped. "I enjoy his company more than yours anyway." She called me back up on the bed and I glared at him defiantly.

Leo rolled his shoulders back as if loosening them up. I hated it when he did that: Things break, boots kick, hands hurt her, and she cries. This time was no different. Words flew back and forth, shouting, angry words. He pulled Jorene to her feet, close to his face, yelling at her.

She closed her eyes, grimacing against the volume of his voice, and shoved him in the chest so hard, she lost her own balance and fell backward.

I didn't mean to do what I did; it was on instinct. Jorene was my pack, and he was threatening her. I jumped up on the bed and sank my teeth into his forearm, right over his new tattoo. My teeth broke skin and he screamed louder than I'd ever heard him scream.

I jumped down to check on Jorene. Distracted, I didn't see his boot, but I felt it when it connected with my rib. I slumped side-ways.

When you're angrier than you are hurt, you become brave. Enough was enough. I jumped up and braced my two front paws firmly on the floor. I pinned my ears back, and bared my teeth. A low, guttural growl reverberated from my chest.

Leo grasped his wounded arm. "He bit me!"

Jorene pulled me to her chest protectively, but instead of watching Leo's boots, I watched his face. Normally, I turned away when he stared at me. Not this time.

"Shh," Jorene said, soothingly stroking my back, trying to calm me, but I wasn't backing down.

Leo stood mute for the first time ever. A flicker of fear crossed his face. He stomped to the bathroom and returned with a towel wrapped around his forearm.

"I'll be back in three days," he sniffed. "I want you and that dawg gone before I return."

She shuffled to her feet, almost tripping on her nightgown. "What do you mean, we have to leave?"

"I'm done!"

She followed him to the kitchen, and I followed her. He collected his six-pack from the counter. "I'll be back Sunday afternoon, and I want it to look like you and that dawg were never here."

"I have nowhere-"

"I don't care." He slammed the door on the way out.

Chapter Three

Three hours passed before Jorene moved from the bed to the living room. I stayed by her side the entire time. She sobbed, yelled at the front door, walked through the house talking out loud, made a couple phone calls, and let me out to go potty.

It was pitch black outside, but I wasn't scared. Tiny white dots scattered across the night sky. The large white ball was up there, just out of reach. When I was a puppy, I would jump as high as I could, trying to grab it, but I never could. I think a few dogs have been able to catch the ball, because I don't always see it.

I enjoyed being outside, still do. But not when it's raining. If it's just a little bit, like the sprinkler Leo would put out in the back yard, I'm okay. But when it comes down hard, with thunder and lightning, I would hide under Jorene's side of the bed.

The tall grass tickled my legs as I sat listening to wind blow through the treetops and the crickets chirp. A small shadow caught my eye as a bullfrog jumped twice and stopped. I tried to taste one once; slimy and bitter. I didn't like it too much and neither did the bullfrog. I never messed with frogs much after that.

The back door hinges creaked and Jorene whistled. "Honeybun, where are you?"

I trotted up to her and she held the door for me to come inside. She got in bed and lifted the blanket and sheet away from her chest. I *never* got under the covers; I always laid on the top.

"It's okay."

That's all the coaxing I needed. I plunged in head first, turned around five times, and settled down with my face on her pillow. This felt great.

"Leo would blow a fuse out of his ears if he saw us right now." A slow grin crossed her face. I smelled stale popcorn as she kissed my nose. "You're the best thing to ever happen to me."

I returned the love with a sloppy kiss, cleaning her wet-salty skin.

"I called Pat, and she'll take us to the bus station Sunday morning," she explained. "I'm going to take care of us. Leo has money hidden in a coffee can in the shop. He doesn't know I know about it. I'm not a thief, but these are extenuating circumstances." She didn't blink, neither did I. "Don't judge me, Honeybun. He owes me, a lot. I figure this is just him paying me back."

◊◊◊

Jorene slept hard, harder than she normally did. It took five minutes to wake her up. I licked her hands, face, and finally, I licked her feet, making her jump and giggle.

She smacked me with Leo's pillow and squealed, "Stop! That tickles."

I chomped on the pillow and a game of tug-of-war began.

"You're such a good boy, yes you are. Get the pillow, come on, get the pillow!"

I bit it and she pulled until the material split and feathers covered the bed and floor. The pillow smelled like Leo, and I ripped it to shreds. Jorene fell across the bed, laughing. I licked her face until she cried for me to stop.

Jorene cried off and on. Each time I comforted her with kisses and cuddled close to her. When her friend Pat arrived, Jorene tried to be strong.

I liked Pat. She always brought me a bone to chew on. She dropped one at my feet when she came inside.

"I'm glad you called me," Pat said, looking around the house. "I just wish it was your decision to leave and on your terms."

"Yeah, well we can't have everything we wish for. Leo has taught me that."

"Don't let that weasel teach you anything, Darling," she hugged Jorene and ruffled my fur. "Let's go pick up your meds."

I was used to being alone in the house, but Jorene had forgotten to let me go potty before she left. I'd drunk an entire bowl of water. Feathers and bones had made me awfully thirsty.

I paced by the front door, waiting for Jorene and Pat to return, but the best view was from the back of the couch looking out the living room window. From this angle, I would see when they drove up. The popcorn I'd eaten over the last day made my stomach hurt.

Where is she? I thought. *Where did she go? When will she be back?*

Frantic, I scratched the back door so hard that paint flaked off. Leo wouldn't be happy with that. I couldn't wait anymore. In a panic, I ran to the couch, knocking over a lamp as I tried to look out the window again. I barely made it off the couch before I peed all over the rug, a huge no-no.

When Jorene came home and examined the back door, her frown hurt worse than Leo's boots ever did. She didn't say a word as she retrieved broken pieces of the lamp from the floor. She tried to scoot me outside, but I didn't have to go anymore. I laid in the living room with my chin on the floor between my paws. Jorene and Pat kicked off their shoes, got comfortable, and chatted.

"He hasn't been good to you for years, Jo," Pat fussed. "If you would-"

"Let's not talk about him," Jorene said. "I need to decide where I'm going."

"Don't you have a cousin in Denver? What was his name, Fred?"

Jorene shook her head. "He doesn't have room, plus he isn't talking to me anymore."

"Why?"

"Why do you think?" Jorene rolled her eyes. "Leo."

"How about your other cousin? You know, the one in Massachusetts?"

"Viola? No, she's allergic to dogs, and I could never leave Honeybun here with Leo." She blew me a kiss and I wagged my tail. I guess she had forgiven me for breaking the lamp and scratching the door.

Jorene stepped on the rug that I peed on. "Oh, Honeybun." She didn't fuss at me often, but I hated hearing my name like she said it at that moment. I tucked my tail and slinked to the other side of the room.

"I can't believe he did this." She ran to the linen closet, came back with a towel, and dabbed my pee spot.

"You really should just leave it there," Pat suggested.

"It could stain it." Jorene kept dabbing.

"Do you really care?"

Jorene slowed down on the dabbing and then stopped all together. She threw down the towel and collapsed on the couch. "I still can't believe I have to leave."

"I'd let you stay at my apartment," Pat said, "but you know they don't allow animals. I tried to sneak a hamster in once and it got loose. It was not a good time for me." She ruffled my fur and my tags clinked against my collar.

Jorene tossed the soiled towel in the laundry. I followed them as they walked to the bedroom.

"What on earth happened in here?" Pat picked up a few feathers.

Jorene tossed her suitcase on the bed. Feathers floated up in the air. "It was a much-needed stress reliever." She crammed her clothes in the suitcase.

"Here." Pat pulled crinkly papers from her pocket and stuffed them in Jorene's back pocket.

"I can't take this." Jorene shook her head, reaching into the back pocket of her jeans. "Besides, I found some extra cash in the house."

Pat grabbed Jorene's wrist, stopping her. "You'll always need more than you have. Take it. Promise me, when you get settled, you'll call and give me your address. I'll help you any time I can."

"I promise."

They talked until early in the morning hours. When I woke up, Pat was on the couch snoring and Jorene slept in a chair with legs dangling over the side. After they ate bagels and drank coffee, I sat by the front door and watched as they went in and out, loading up Pat's car.

Jorene was quiet as Pat talked nonstop. Jorene slipped her medication in her purse.

"Okay, I think I have everything." She walked through the house and I followed behind. She'd already cleaned up the feathers and started making the bed before Pat came in.

"Are you kidding me?" Pat stood with her hands on her hips. "You're actually making his bed?"

They stared at each other. I sat at Jorene's feet, waiting.

Jorene ripped the covers and sheets from the bed and left them in a pile on the floor. In the kitchen, Jorene popped open three beers and drained them down the sink. She left the refrigerator door ajar, just like the front door when we walked out.

◊◊◊

As Pat pulled up at the bus stop, Jorene attached the leash to my collar. The collar didn't bother me anymore, but the leash was torture.

"Be still." Jorene fussed as I fidgeted at the end of the leash.

If I kept pace with her strides, I didn't feel the resistance as much, but she kept changing her speed.

While Pat bought the bus ticket and Jorene was distracted, I peed on a flower growing between the cracks in the concrete.

"Honeybun!" Jorene jerked my leash.

Pat laughed. "Be sure to call me as soon as you settle down for the night."

"I promise. I'll probably head south. Leo hates Florida. He always says it's too hot and he doesn't like being outside. I've heard the beaches are amazing, and I've always wanted to see them."

Many people were waiting for the bus with Jorene and Pat. One little lady slipped me a piece of chicken. I sat close to her for a while, hoping for more, but she finished it herself.

A bus screeched to a stop, spewing fumes, and several people stepped out of it. Jorene and Pat hugged. I wasn't sure how to climb up in the bus, and people behind us grumbled with impatience. Someone stepped on my tail and I yelped. Jorene picked me up and carried me up the steps. She pulled me close and whispered in my ear. "Don't you dare pee in this bus."

She didn't have to worry; I already peed on the flower.

"And watch out for the gum on the floor," she added.

We sat in the first empty seat, two rows behind the bus driver.

The driver looked back over his shoulder and frowned. "Lady, no dogs are allowed on here." He tapped a sign above his head that showed a dog with a line drawn across it.

"He's a therapy dog. I forgot his vest."

Jorene patted the seat beside her. I jumped up on the seat by the window. It was a bumpy ride, and the old man in the seat in front of us snored louder than Pat. He smelled of cheese and crackers. When Jorene dozed, I squeezed through the area between the window and his seat. It only took a moment to clean the cracker and cheese crumbles from his shirt.

It was when I tried to get the last piece of cheese stuck in his beard that the driver hit the curb. I lost my balance and fell deeper in the crevice between the seats. I panicked and yelped, waking Jorene and cheese-n-crackers man.

"I'm so sorry, sir." Jorene pulled me free and I curled up beside her. I was hungry, and those crumbs only made me hungrier. I wondered if Leo had eaten my honey buns.

It was a long ride to this place called Florida. We changed buses a few times and ate weird-tasting food at the bus stop.

Jorene stroked my back. "I know you're tired, but we're so close. This is the last bus, I promise." She tapped the shoulder of the man sitting in front of us. "Excuse me, sir. Where is the closest beach?"

He cleared his throat. "Head south to the Panhandle, there's several beaches. My cousin, Bobby, lives on the Wakulla River, but you want the beach, huh?" He scratched his chin. "You could try Panacea beach. It's pretty quiet there, unless they're having a festival. If you want to be where there are lots of people, try St. George Island or Panama City Beach."

Jorene smiled. "Thank you. I'm not interested in lots of people. Panacea sounds perfect."

Chapter Four

Jorene wasn't happy when she learned the bus route didn't go to Panacea. We hitchhiked the rest of the way.

A truck with vinyl decals on the doors reading "Gator-Grip Towing" stopped to pick us up. An old, rough-looking man loaded up her luggage. He smelled like fish and old shoes.

"You are sitting between us," Jorene whispered in my ear, just before wedging me between the driver and herself.

"What kinda dog you got thar?" the stranger asked. Even though he smelled wonderful, I leaned away from him, against Jorene.

"I think he's a Carolina Dog. That's what my husband believes."

"Mighty fine-lookin' dog."

"You can drop us off at the first gas station, please. I have a friend I'm meeting."

The man nodded. I didn't know of any friends that we had in Panacea.

As the man unloaded his truck in the gas station parking lot, he asked Jorene for her number.

She handed him a five-dollar bill. "This is the only number I'm giving you, thanks."

"Watch out for bears," the man grumbled as he got back in his truck and slammed the door. Pebbles and dirt shot up in our faces as he sped away.

"Well, that was uncalled-for," Jorene said. She brushed the dirt from her clothing and found a discarded newspaper on a bench outside of the gas station. I wasn't sure what she was looking for, but she kept circling things.

After a few minutes, she put down her pen and took a deep breath, and a couple coughs followed. When they subsided, she said, "Honeybun, don't let that man frighten you with his talk about bears. We'll probably never see one." She cleared her throat. "But if we do, don't try to be the hero, you hear me? For the most part, they mind their own business, but if you get on their bad side, they could rip you to shreds with one swipe of a paw. Just leave it be and it will go away."

She took another deep breath and smiled when it wasn't followed by a cough. We got up and went inside the store.

"May I use your phone, please?"

I walked in circles around her, twisting the leash tight against her legs.

"We don't allow dogs in here, so make it quick." The man slid the phone across the counter to Jorene. Hotdogs rolled over and over on a rack on the counter. A puddle of my drool soaked my front paws, and I didn't even care.

The man tossed a dirty washcloth over the counter onto the floor. "You'll need to clean that up."

She circled the cloth over the drool on the floor with her shoe while she spoke into the phone. "Yes, I'm calling about a camper for sale?"

The man behind the counter threw me a hotdog as we were leaving. I caught it mid-air.

"We're meeting a lady in ten minutes. She has a camper for sale and it's all set up and ready." Jorene sat on the bench outside and I looked through the glass door, wishing the guy would throw me another hotdog. "It's a fresh start, for both of us."

◊◊◊

"How do you like our new home, Honeybun?" Jorene asked as she walked around the camper, opening and closing cabinet doors. It was smaller than our house in South Carolina, but there was no Leo. This is perfect, just what I was looking for." She opened up a small white refrigerator. Curious, I inched closer. It was empty.

"It looks like it will only hold about three days' worth of food."

At the mention of food my stomach rumbled.

"I know, I know. I need to get some groceries."

We stepped outside. Many campers of various sizes, shapes, and colors lined the driveways. Ours was right by the water. I jogged past a picnic table and a round pit encircled by stones to the sandy shore and drank deeply. I jerked my head back and hawked the water back up.

Jorene pulled me back. "That's salt water. You can't drink it."

She kicked off her flip-flops and stepped in the water. "It's not really a beach, not like you see on postcards, but this is fine for me, as long as we're out of South Carolina."

Jorene walked in the water and I stayed close to her on the sand. She splashed me and I tried to bite the water in the air before it touched me. She laughed harder than I'd ever heard her laugh.

I met lots of dogs in the campground. Some wanted to play, others barked and growled at me. I stayed right by Jorene the entire day. I was only interested in food and being with her.

"Hi, I'm Belle." A woman approached us on a bicycle. I'd seen one of these two-wheeled things before. I'd gotten a close-up look once when I chased one, caught it, and then got pulled under the front wheel. One encounter with a bicycle was enough for me. I stood on the far side of Jorene, keeping my eyes trained on the bicycle.

They chatted a few minutes and walked over to Belle's camper. An older bicycle with a basket attached in front of the handlebars leaned against the side of the camper. Jorene gave Belle some crinkly papers while I sniffed the bicycle's tires and peed on one of them.

"What did I tell you, Honeybun? Life is looking good."

I'd never seen her ride a bicycle before. She fell twice, brushed the dirt from her hands and knees, and kept trying. I pulled the leash taut as I walked down the road alongside her.

Within a few minutes, Jorene was riding smoothly, and I gradually relaxed, realizing that she wouldn't run over me. I smelled food...all kinds of food: Hotdogs, fish, hamburgers, bread, and soups. And the drooling started.

A long row of tents lined the road, and crowds of people walked around. "Oh, it's a Farmer's Market!" Jorene walked her bike from one tent to the next while I sniffed the ground, gobbling up a French fry and a piece of hamburger bun along the way.

We came home with towels and bedding in the bicycle's basket and plastic bags filled with fresh bread, meats, vegetables, and drinks tied to the handlebars.

That night, we were invited across the way by our new neighbors to enjoy some food on the grill. Jorene laughed and talked with them almost as much as she did when Pat visited. The laughing made her cough more, but she seemed happier than I'd ever seen her.

After we ate and said goodnight to everyone, Jorene collected small twigs and branches, dropping them in the round pit of stones. It took her a little while to get a fire lit, but once she created a spark it roared to life. She pulled a couple logs away to lessen the heat. I settled down in the warm sand at her feet and listened to the fire pop and hiss.

Most everyone had turned in for the night, and the campground had grown dark.

"If you listen carefully, you can hear the water rolling up just a few yards away." Jorene ran her fingers through my fur, scratching the nape of my neck. "They even have shuffleboard and a pool here! It's like a permanent holiday."

◊◊◊

She showered before we went to bed. I licked water that splashed on the floor so she wouldn't slip getting out, and as a thank you, she let me curl up on the bed with her.

"Guess what? The nice people at the Farmer's Market said they could use some extra help. I can even bring you with me so you won't be stuck inside." She sighed and hugged me tight.

I inched up so my nose touched her chin, watching as she closed her eyes. Her breath smelled of hamburger, French fries, and something new that I couldn't place. I didn't like this new scent. It always smelled stronger when she coughed.

"I didn't lie to the bus driver. You've been my therapy dog since the day I fell in love with you."

Life for us was good…until it wasn't.

Chapter Five

We'd been living in the camper for about four years. I'd seen people come and go. Big dogs, little dogs, yippy dogs, friendly dogs, even a few cats on leashes. It was the strangest thing I'd ever seen. I enjoyed chasing the cats, but the people holding onto the other end of their leashes didn't like it too much.

We always relaxed outside the camper if the mosquitoes, yellow flies, and no-see-ums weren't bad. Jorene loved walking on the little sandy strip of beach by the campers. Sometimes she'd take me over the bridge to the big beach to look for shells, but I liked our small beach better.

I saw some strange things crawling around on our beach: Creatures with more legs than me and even creatures with no legs. I even saw people pull fish out of the water. The fish gave it their all, splashed, jumped in the air, but in the end, most of them ended up on shore. They fought the fishing line like I used to fight the leash. Neither one of us won, but I had a better fate than them.

One of the highlights of living at the campground was grease. I'd lick the delicious drippings from Jorene's grill as soon as they hit the ground. I stole a hotdog or two from the grill too, but she never fussed much about it.

Jorene had always talked to me, but since we'd moved to Panacea, she talked to me constantly about everything. I can't read or write, but I always listened and watched what she pointed at when she talked.

I learned a lot from her. I learned that the white dots in the night sky are called stars and the large white ball is called Moon. The big bright ball in the daylight that hurts my eyes when I stare at it is called Sun. Those strange walking shells on the beach are crabs, the slimy things on the beach with no legs are jellyfish, and the large birds with saggy necks are pelicans.

Jorene always dragged me away from the jellyfish, but curiosity drew me to them. They smelled awful and great at the same time.

Jorene's cough visited her more often. One time, I noticed red stuff in her hand when she coughed, like I saw on Leo's arm when I bit him. "I'm fine; I just need to rest a bit." She said that a lot back then. She pedaled her bicycle slower and stopped frequently to rest, even if we were only going for a ten-minute ride to the Farmer's Market where she worked. I didn't mind, I knew we'd get to where we were going, eventually. I wasn't in a hurry.

"I'm so glad you're with me. The last four years, I've been the happiest I've ever been." She kissed my nose that night and held me tight as she drifted off to sleep.

The next morning, I wasn't able to wake her up. I tried everything. I licked her face, whined, pulled at the covers, and eventually I barked loudly in her ear. She didn't like getting woken up like that, but nothing else was working. She didn't flinch. Something was wrong.

I ran to the doggy door, but she'd closed the flap and locked it for the night. I barked and scratched at it. Campers were waking up and moving around outside; maybe I could get their attention.

I ran back to our bed, jumped up, and slid my snout just under the edge of the partially opened window. I barked as loud and as long as I could.

A couple guys tried to open the front door, but it was locked. I jumped and scratched the door trying to help, but couldn't get it open either. When they walked away, I howled.

I rammed the door, shaking the camper. It gave me a headache and only made a small dent in the door. I ran back to the window above our bed and watched the two guys talking to the handyman, Ricky. I heard one of them say, "Something's wrong with Jorene."

"Jorene, are you in there?" Ricky yelled through the door, jiggling the door knob.

"Her bicycle is still here. She must be home," another guy said.

I'd often watched Ricky working on campers, and when I saw the tip of a screwdriver jut in between the door and door frame, I knew he was trying to get it open. He pulled, twisted, and bent part of the door around the knob.

I tried to grab the screwdriver with my teeth to help, but couldn't get hold of it. Jorene was going to be so angry about her door when they woke her up.

The door flew open with a whoosh.

I barked, jumped, and ran back to Jorene as Ricky and the other two guys rushed in.

A lady pushed the men aside and touched Jorene's face. "Jo, are you okay?" She touched Jorene's wrist, closed her eyes, and frowned.

I moved closer to Jorene. Something was different. With all these people and all the barking and noise I caused, she just hadn't woken up.

That's the day my life changed. Jorene was taken from me. I was inconsolable. I growled and barked at everyone who tried to touch her. Ricky threw a blanket over me and scooped me up. He shoved me in another person's camper across from mine and Jorene's.

The only way to see my camper was if I climbed up on their table to look out the window. Jorene would be upset with me for misbehaving. She fussed at me once when I jumped up on our table and pulled a turkey to the floor. She'd just taken it out of the oven and it burned my tongue. I barely made it outside with a turkey leg in my mouth when she tried to pop my rear with a wet wash cloth.

This time, I didn't care. A van with flashing lights on its roof pulled into the campground. Men in white suits walked into my camper. They came out carrying Jorene on a bed with wheels. She had a sheet over her face, but I knew it was her. We used to play a game where she hid under the sheet and called my name, "Come and find me, Honeybun." I always found her.

The camper Ricky locked me in didn't have a doggie door, like in my camper. I tore up everything: The bed, pillows, blankets, curtains. It wasn't until I knocked over the dishes, that everyone outside heard the noise. When the door opened, I darted out and ran in the direction of the big white van with flashing lights. I didn't see them on the road. There were too many other cars in the way, but I was pretty sure I knew which way they went. I ran until I saw the sun dropping low in the sky, but I never did find that van.

I had run a long way. Nothing looked familiar. The trees were different, the road was wider, and sounds in the woods were strange. Cars that drove by were not the cars I always saw at the Farmer's Market or the campground. They honked their horns, scaring me. I walked in the tall grass on the side of the road, not sure where I was going. It was weird not having Jorene guide me with the leash.

The ground even felt different. I was used to seeing tall slender grass growing out of white sand with broken shells on the ground. This ground was dark brown with thick stubby grass. How far had I run from home? I wasn't sure which way to go, except to try and follow my old trail.

By nightfall, thirst and hunger were the only things on my mind. I missed the warmth of the bed with Jorene. On instinct, I turned toward a dim light in the woods. Maybe it was her. Maybe the van was there. The small dim light was a night light on a house, like the one by the door on our camper. That meant people were there, maybe. Drool dribbled down my jowls at the scent of food. I stopped just before a clearing and hid behind a bush. I watched and listened to two men standing near a grill outside the house.

"I'm telling you, Wade, if that man hadn't of stopped flirting with Sandy, I'd a knocked his *other* front tooth out. Hand me a few of those hotdog buns." The first man flipped the hotdogs. I crept closer.

"Tully, how long have you been living out here on Spring Hill Road?" Wade asked. He grabbed a handful of chips from a bag on a table near the grill.

Tully turned the hot dogs over. "Oh, maybe three years now."

"All by yourself, you never worry about bears 'round here?" Wade belched. "I hear there have been a few large ones."

"Nope, it's always quiet around here." Tully reached for the hotdog buns.

"At least think about gettin' a dog or something. Huntin' season is almost here. You could use a good huntin' dog."

My plan was to wait until they went inside and steal that bag of chips and any extra hotdogs lying around, but something hooted behind me and I jumped. Tully and Wade stared in my direction.

Wade reached over and grabbed something off the table.

"What are you going to do with that spatula? You gonna smack a bear on the rear?" Tully said, laughing.

I tried to creep away without a sound, but stepped on a twig. It cracked, giving me away.

"Okay, something is r-really out there and it's w-watching us," Wade stammered, tensing.

Tully stared right at me, but I was sure he couldn't see me. Could he? Then his face softened.

"Hey, buddy, come on, are you hungry?" He held out a hotdog and whispered something to Wade.

Wade held out a hotdog too. "You lost, fella?"

So, here I was, starving, and two strangers were trying to feed me hotdogs. My stomach made the decision for me. I stepped out of the shadows, one paw at a time, stopping when their porch light shone on me.

"Oh, you're a bigger fella than I thought," Tully said. "How about three hotdogs?" He held out two along with the one Wade offered. They looked like nice men, but ever since Leo, I'd always been leery of men, especially men in boots. I've always liked women better. They had softer voices and were gentler. I missed Jorene.

"It's okay. Come on. I won't bite," Tully coaxed.

"Speaking of huntin' dogs."

Tully shook his head. "This ain't a huntin' dog. Not the right breed. Looks sort of like the wild dogs my dad used to talk about that live up in Georgia and South Carolina."

I crept closer, watching the hotdogs dangle from Wade's hand.

"See that collar and tags?" Tully asked. "He's someone's pet."

Wade shrugged. "Well, you could keep him as yours."

The hotdogs glistened with juices. Just a few more steps and I could snatch one. *Better not try to grab me.* Quick as a flash, I lunged and took one, my teeth just missing Tully's fingers.

"Whoa, easy there, fella." Tully looked at his hand to make sure he still had all his fingers.

I barely remember tasting those hotdogs. They were down in two gulps. I sat down, waiting for more.

"Toss him yours, Wade."

Wade shifted in his seat, leaned forward, and then hesitated. "We have more, right?"

Tully rolled his eyes. "Just do it."

Wade tossed me the hotdog and I ate it faster than the first two.

"I've never seen him around here. I'm at least ten miles from any other houses, if not more," Tully said. "I'm surprised someone didn't hit him if he came from Spring Hill. I see road-kill all the time on that road: Deer, stray cats and dogs."

"He looks too healthy to be a stray. He's probably just lost. I'll see if I can read his tags." When Wade stood up and walked toward me, I ran back into the woods.

"Man, why'd you do that? You spooked him."

"It's just some homeless dog. You gave him a good meal. I'm sure he'll head home now. Throw a few more on the grill." Wade sat back down and the chair creaked.

Tully walked through the clearing to the edge of the woods looking for me. "Hey, I have another hotdog. Come and get it!"

I stayed beyond the tree line and didn't move until Tully gave up and went back to the house. Every once in a while, he scanned the tree line for me, but I stayed hidden and settled down on some pine straw to take a nap. It was nice to hear human voices, but I didn't want those men to touch me.

Chapter Six

Their chairs were empty in the morning and the trailer lights were out. Two bowls were on the ground by the grill: One with cold water and the other with hotdogs and potato salad. I'd be seeing Tully again if he continued to leave food like this out for me. I ate quickly and took a long drink of water before I headed for the main road. I stepped off onto the grass each time a car drove by. The grass was dewy and I didn't like the way it felt on my feet. The road felt better for walking and kept my feet dry. I walked in the direction I knew by instinct led to the campground.

To a dog there isn't too much that stinks, but that night, one smell stood above all others that I'd ever smelled and it stank something awful. The odor was so strong it made my nose wrinkle. I couldn't tell where it came from until an oncoming car's headlights hit it. A black animal with a white stripe down its back lay on the side of the road, dead. I must have run three miles before I couldn't smell it anymore.

Someone threw a half-eaten hamburger out their car window as they passed me. I ate it along with most of the wrapper covered in melted cheese.

The ground trembled as I swallowed the last bite. A large tan animal bounded over me, followed by three more. They jumped from one side of the road to the other, their hooves touching the road only once. They had long skinny legs and something that looked like branches coming out of their heads

35

between their ears. I had seen deer in South Carolina, but they had never jumped right over me. Just as quickly as they appeared, they melted into the woods, their upturned white tails flashing briefly before they disappeared. Here one second and gone the next.

When the sun came up, I was still walking, barely. The ground wasn't brown anymore, but sandy, like the beach where we lived. A car drove by and I recognized it. It was Shelley, a neighbor who lived in the campground. I must be near home! My feet came alive and I chased after her. I couldn't see the car any more, but the Farmer's Market was within sight.

I trotted up to the booth that Jorene worked at. Maybe she would be there. Maybe she was okay.

"Hey, guys, Honeybun is here." Stephanie was Jorene's boss. She gave me pickles to eat one time. They were awful, but she's all right, I guess. Shelley wasn't around.

"You know, you have someone looking for you. Her name is Pat." Stephanie reached out to touch me, but I pulled away. "Just as I figured, but I always have to try." Stephanie placed a bowl of water at my feet and I drank until the bowl was dry.

My favorite spot to relax was under the table at Stephanie's vegetable stand. I crawled under it, hidden from everyone as the red and white checkered tablecloth flapped in the breeze. I fell asleep while Stephanie talked to customers about farm-fresh tomatoes and the banana bread she had made *just this morning*.

Hours later, when I woke up, Stephanie had packed up her vegetable stand. She pulled the tablecloth off the table to fold it and I stretched. She squatted down in front of me. "I'm sorry to hear about Jorene. I know she loved you very much. I wish I could keep you, but I can't."

Keep me? Why would you keep me? I have an owner, Jorene.

Stephanie stood up, shaking her head. "It's so sad. When someone dies it even affects the pets."

Dies? Who died? I thought of Jorene lying on the bed, not moving, and the skunk on the side of the road, not moving. That's when I knew I would never see Jorene again. I stayed under that table the rest of the day after Stephanie packed up and left. Where was I to go? The camper! The camper had a soft bed and food. I ran in the direction of home.

◊◊◊

Several men moved in and out of our camper. They loaded our stuff in a van. Pat was there! I ran to her and tried to get her to stop the men.

"Oh, sweetie, there you are. Slow down. I know you miss her, but it's going to be okay." She kept trying to get her hand on my collar, but I dodged out of her reach. She disappeared inside my camper and came out with my leash. When she stepped toward me, I ran in the opposite direction and hid under a camper at the far end of the campground.

"Honeybun, come on, we can't stay here." She walked all over that campground for most of the afternoon, calling to me and searching for me, while I watched as they packed up Jorene's and my home.

"Lady, we're leaving now. Where do you want us to take this stuff?" the van driver asked.

Tears ran down Pat's face. She looked around desperately. "I just need a little longer. I have to find her dog."

I considered coming out. Pat had always been nice to me, but that leash was in her hand so I stayed hidden.

"Honeybun, please!" she cried.

"Lady…," the man persisted.

"Okay, just get in the truck. I'm coming."

Pat whistled for me, but I wasn't budging. "I can't stay any longer. Please come out." She walked to her car and sat in it for a minute with the engine cranked.

The guy in the van honked the horn and then they both pulled away.

I ran to our camper. The door was ajar and I stepped inside. The last time I'd seen it this clean and empty was when Jorene first bought it. Everything was gone except the mattress and refrigerator. Even my food and water bowls were gone. So were all the familiar sounds: The can opener whirring when Jorene opened my food, her laughter as we played tug-of-war, her singing while she washed dishes.

I crawled up on the bare mattress. The scent of Jorene comforted me. No one came to check on me that night, but that was okay. I didn't want to be with anyone. Sleep came quickly.

When I woke up later that night, I couldn't see anything at first and didn't remember where I was. I smelled Jorene's scent on the mattress and it all came back. I laid my head back down and whimpered. Stars shone through the window by our bed and crickets chirped. This was the time of the evening when we would sit outside watching the stars and moon, enjoying a bonfire. Sometimes we walked to the water.

I nudged the door open and sat in the sand outside, watching the campers. They moved about, cooking, visiting, and laughing as if nothing had changed. Jorene's place was dark and quiet. I sulked to the beach. Crabs saw me coming and scurried away. I almost had one, but it ran into the water and I lost sight of it.

"Is that you there, Honeybun?" a voice called from one of the campers.

One of our neighbors, Agnes, stood outside her camper, watching me. I walked farther down the beach into the darkness, escaping her eyes. I didn't want to stay with her. She was nice, but her kids teased me.

The granddaddy of all crabs stood high up on the shore line, motionless. I was sure I could get it before it reached the water, so I ran for it. Pain shot through my paw when I stumbled in the dark on a jellyfish. Jorene had been right to pull me away from them. My paw was stung and burned.

I limped back to the camper, slipped through the open door, and crawled up on the mattress where I knew I was safe; no jellyfish, no stinky, black-and white animals, no jumping animals with branches in their heads, and no Pat with a leash. I licked my stinging paw until I fell asleep.

Chapter Seven

A week had passed since Jorene was taken from me. Her scent faded from the mattress. Someone tried to take more stuff out of our home, but I stood with my hackles up and my teeth bared. They didn't come back.

Our neighbors started leaving scraps for me to eat: burgers, hot dogs, chicken, and once in a while, dog food. I drank from a dripping spigot near the campground's pool. I wondered if I could find my way back to my mother.

People shuffled around outside the camper. "Have you seen that dog?" one guy asked.

"Not this morning. I'm sure if he's in there, he'll come running out once this is hooked up."

The camper shifted a little and the sound of something being peeled away from the bottom of the camper hurt my ears. I climbed up on the mattress and looked out the window. I couldn't see the men, but I heard everything they were doing.

"Okay, she's ready! Let's go," one guy yelled.

The ground under my feet shook as the camper moved. I thought it was being ripped apart. The ground in front of me was moving! I darted out and tripped on my own paws, falling face first in the sand. I blinked as the sand irritated my eyes and blurred my vision.

A huge truck dragged my home away. First they took Jorene, and then they took my home. I ran as fast as I could after the camper, but right as I was within jumping distance of getting in the camper, they pulled onto the highway and sped up.

I was thirsty, tired, and alone on the side of the road. At least this time, I knew the way back home. I'd traveled this way when I chased the white van with flashing lights, only I didn't go as far as I did that time.

I wasn't sure what to do. I was used to being alone and taking care of myself, but I'd always had a home. I turned in the only direction I knew, Panacea. At least it was a familiar place, and I might find food and water.

Half-way to the campground, I spotted another dog. You can't trust a dog, that's the honest truth. The ones at the campground come and go. I'd never been one to make friends easily. This dog was the largest one I'd ever seen. It was twice my size and I'm not small. Black shaggy hair hung over his eyes and his matted tail hair had twigs entwined. No collar on his neck indicated he was a stray like me. Homeless dogs are never to be trusted; they don't have any fear. I'm an exception in this respect.

He didn't see me at first. A bag that someone tossed out their car window held his interest. But the moment his eyes met mine, I knew it would be trouble. His interest went to a whole new level. He held his tail high, wagged it twice, and then stood erect. His front legs spread out in a stiff stance and he lowered his head to shoulder level.

I knew that look. I'd seen it before with a few dogs at the campground. He was trying to determine if I was a threat to whatever was in the bag. Trust me; I'm not a threat. The bag was the last thing on my mind. Most campers with aggressive dogs like this one, left after a few days when other campers complained.

If I ran, I'd be an easy target, so I stood my ground. We stared at each other for a long time. Eventually, he must have determined I wasn't a threat. He resumed inspecting the contents of the bag.

I laid down to wait until he left. I didn't want to take a chance of being chased. With his long, powerful legs, he'd catch up and tear into me in no time.

When he finished examining the bag, he raised his head in my direction, scratched his back legs in the dirt, shooting grass behind him, and huffed at me before trotting off.

After sniffing the bag to see if the other dog had left anything for me to eat, I continued on my way. I was almost home. My body ached, but a familiar scent filled the air: Moisture mingled with dirt, grass, and other animals. I raised my head to the scent. Tree tops quivered and leaves rustled in small eddies on the ground. I knew this scent: rain.

I quickened my pace. The first rumble came from the sky and the sun had hidden behind a dark grey cloud. I hated being caught in the rain. I picked up speed, trying to outrun the dark clouds that spread above me.

The wind picked up and the first rain drops hit my nose and muzzle. The entire sky lit up, flashing before my eyes. I dodged off the road into the woods, running between the pine trees and searching for somewhere to hide until the storm passed.

I crawled under an old rusty car abandoned in the middle of the woods. A small brown and white rabbit that had found refuge under the car darted out into the rain. It disappeared into the woods.

Lying under the car in the warm dry dirt, I watched thin rivers of water flow under the car. I withdrew my paws to avoid getting them wet.

Each time the sky clapped with thunder and lightning, I squeezed my eyes closed. The storm wasn't stopping. I withdrew farther under the car to where the rivers of water couldn't reach me and curled up in a tight ball.

◊◊◊

Rays of morning sunshine filtered through leaves above, casting an early morning glow on the ground. I'd slept a long time and woke up stiff to my bones. A rank smell hit me in the face. Four gigantic hairy legs the diameter of small trees circled the car. Black claws the width of Tully's hotdogs jutted out from the creature's paws. Even if a mountain of honey buns was out there, I wouldn't have left the shelter of the car. I belly crawled to the other side of the vehicle and tried to make myself as small and invisible as possible.

The creature poked its black nose under the car. I'd never seen anything like it in my life. Not in the woods in South Carolina and not here in Panacea, Florida. But from what Jorene had told me, I knew this was a bear. Its small black eyes stared menacingly. Its breath smelled like something rotten. I felt the vibrations in my bones when the bear roared within inches of my face.

Instinctively, I barked in defense. I shouldn't have done that, because it angered the bear even more. It clawed at the dirt to get under the car, plowing up long rows of tilled earth. It had more room to get to me now.

It was now or never. I was sure to be a dead dog if that thing got me. I crawled from side to side as fast as I could to confuse it. Between the two of us, we stirred up so much dust I couldn't see where he was, but I could hear him. I crawled out as fast as I could from the other side of the car and barreled toward the highway.

A truck was parked on the side of the road. A man stood at the front of the truck and slammed the hood down.

"Okay, Kelly-Ruth, try starting it now," he yelled.

The engine roared to life. I jumped up in the bed of the truck and hid behind an old spare tire as the truck pulled onto the highway. I looked back to see if the creature followed. It emerged from the woods looking confused but didn't give chase.

I found part of a hamburger discarded in the corner of the truck bed. I ate it and tried to lick the melted cheese off the wrapper, but ended up eating the whole thing, wrapper and all. I turned around and leaned against the tire, watching and listening through their half-opened window to see where we were going.

The man leaned over and kissed the woman. That's when he saw me.

"We got ourselves a hitch-hiker in the back."

The woman turned around and a huge grin appeared on her face. "Ahh, Justin, he's precious. I wonder how he got back there. Should we pull over?"

"I'm getting gas two miles up the road. I don't want to take a chance of the truck not starting again until we get to a mechanic's shop."

She nodded. "Okay. He has a collar and tags. Probably someone's missing a pet. I'll check his tags when we stop."

So, there I sat, with the lady making googly eyes at me and talking to me like Jorene did when I was a puppy. Despite being annoyed at her voice, my tail wagged in response to her friendly tone. I hated when that happened.

The truck sputtered as we pulled into the gas station. I'd been here before. Cooper, the guy that cooked in the back, always gave me sausages. I just needed to bark twice and scratch once on the back door.

I jumped from the truck bed and disappeared behind the building.

"Where is he?" Kelly-Ruth asked.

"I don't know. Maybe he jumped out before we got here. We couldn't have kept him, anyway," Justin answered. "They don't allow dogs at the rental property."

I barked once and scratched twice. Cooper opened the door.

"I ain't got time to chat. We've been busy, but I saved this for you." He tossed me a couple of sausage patties. "Next time, don't bark. If Mel finds outs that I've been giving you food, he'll fire me. Remember the code I said to use? Two scratches, no barks. See you next week." He winked and slammed the door.

I wasn't in the mood to sit and listen to anyone talk right now anyway. I just wanted a sausage for the road. I knew of a better place.

Chapter Eight

I scratched the back door and sat down to wait. The metal door creaked open on rusty hinges.

"Well lookie here. I wondered when you'd be back." Miles looked down at me. He wiped his hands on the white apron that hung loosely from his waist. He smelled of fish and hushpuppies. If there was ever someone I'd snuggle with beside Jorene, it might be Miles, just because he smelled so good.

"Here ya go, old boy." Miles leaned over, put a handful of fried food scraps on the back steps, and wiped his greasy fingers on his apron again. He'd tried a few times to convince me to take food from his hand. Not a chance, not happening again. Not since I accidentally nipped his finger a week ago when he gave me some shrimp. His fingers and the shrimp smelled the same. After that, he placed the food on the steps. He disappeared inside and came back out with a bowl of water.

"I heard about Jorene. Sorry to hear about that, Sport. I always enjoyed chatting with you two when you'd come by for lunch." He scratched his furry chin. "You know, there are a lot of people lookin' for you. I thought maybe you'd run away. I ain't seen you in a while." He reached down to pet me. I stepped backward just out of reach.

"Yeah, I didn't think so. You never did care much for people touching you, except for Jorene. I guess the sound of our voices and food is enough. Gotta get back to work, ole boy."

The sky rumbled and we both looked up.

"Better get somewhere dry, but come back later and I'll bring you a seafood platter with extra hushpuppies." The metal door slammed behind him.

I drank the water and sat on the step for a few minutes, watching clouds move across the sky. I trotted down the road in the opposite direction of the dark clouds. A large truck swerved, wheels screeched, horns honked, and people yelled. I ran toward the woods.

Usually I'm a good judge of how much time I have to get away from the rain and thunder, but this storm came up fast. Rain pelted my back hard and rolled down my face, blurring my vision. If not for a flash of lightning, I wouldn't have seen the old house nestled in the woods. I crawled under the porch where it was dry, but was quickly forced out by a mother raccoon and her babies. She hissed at me and her four babies ran farther under the house. I jumped up on the porch and pushed the partially closed door open just enough for me to squeeze in.

Houses meant people and lots of noise, but this house was quiet and empty except for one piece of furniture in the living room: a couch with the side chewed up. It smelled of other animals. Some were dog smells, but most I didn't recognize. Newspapers and trash littered the floor, but the house was dry and safe; that's all I needed.

I decided to look around. In the kitchen, all the cabinet doors hung open. An upper door barely hung on by one hinge and a lower one leaned against the wall where the refrigerator should have been. No food in sight, not even a crumb on the counters.

The bedrooms were empty except for a coat hanging in a closet. I pulled the coat from the hanger with my teeth and carried it back to the living room, placing it on the couch. With the coat bunched up on top, I didn't feel the spring poking me. Once I settled down, I feel fast asleep.

◊◊◊

"Oh, Honeybun, there you are. I've been looking everywhere for you!"

That was Jorene's voice! *She's back, she's back!* I ran into her open arms and she squeezed so tight that it hurt, but I didn't care. I licked every part of her face, ears, nose, and neck. She was finally home. "I missed you so much," she said with a smile. I howled in excitement.

That's what woke me up, my own howling. I blinked and looked around. No Jorene. I was in the old abandoned house, sleeping on a worn-out-couch, a spring jabbing my side. A small white mouse stood on the back of the couch staring at me. It dove under the cushions when I stood up.

My collar, the last remnants of being owned by someone, snapped and fell onto the couch when I shook the sleep off. Jorene always struggled to get me to keep that collar on. My neck was now free from the annoying clanging of the tags. I jumped off the couch, shook again, and scratched my neck. Finally, I was able to scratch all the itchy spots.

I was alone, except for a scared mouse, but I had a roof over my head, a couch to sleep on, and no one was trying to catch me. That's all I really needed. My new home was right here.

The sun was high in the sky, drying the saturated ground when I arrived at the campground. The no-see-ums were horrible. Their favorite parts of me are my ears, eyes, and nose, with the exception of my rear. I sat down quickly during no-see-um season, but they bothered me less when I moved.

◊◊◊

Residents at the campground appeared happy to see me and tossed me leftovers. This had become routine for me. I knew how to take care of myself, who to trust, and who to avoid. I also knew who to visit to get good food and who to skip – the ones that offered me dog-food. The occasional conversation with people wasn't too bad, either. I made my own rules and wasn't held captive by a collar and leash.

Yeah, life wasn't too bad.

Chapter Nine

No telling how long I'd lived on the streets. I'd seen a few winters and summers. I'd seen wind rip up a pine tree from its roots and plant it inside a house. Two or three times a year, people cheered and celebrated when the sky exploded with colors, and I ran to the next county to escape the awful noise. All the people I knew, when Jorene and I lived there, moved on or weren't working at the Farmer's Market anymore. Even the campers we became friends with didn't come to the campground anymore.

I'd seen rain pounding the ground so hard that it bounced back up in my nose. Sometimes, the asphalt burned my paws; other times I thought I was walking on ice. Yellow flies ranked first in my list of annoyances –even above the no-see-ums. I'd do just about anything to get away from yellow flies.

Some mornings, I sat on the dock at the campground. The sunrise was just a soft yellow glow through the fog, and the sound of the birds flying by was my only clue that they were leaving and wouldn't return until sunset. If I was lucky, the cool breezes scattered the no-see-ums before they found me.

Once, I tried to cross the big bridge near the campground. I remembered Jorene taking me to a beach on the other side. Maybe I'd find her there. But the cars drove too fast and too close for my comfort. Dirt and small pebbles shot up in my face from a spinning tire and stung my eyes, and one truck almost hit me. I didn't even make it to the top of the bridge before turning around.

Whenever I was bored with the leftovers from the campers, I trotted down the road and visited a nice old lady. She always rocked in a chair on her front porch, sipped sweat tea, and watched cars drive by. "Old Fluella's got a treat for you," she'd say. She'd reach into a greasy paper sack on the floor and pull out a tasty treat. She fed me fish and mountains of hushpuppies from the restaurant Miles worked at. I ate until my belly was so swollen that all I could do was sit next to her rocker and help her watch cars drive by.

Walking was difficult for Fluella, and eventually a young man named Clyde moved in to take care of her. I didn't get hushpuppies everyday like before, but I think he worked at a pizza place, because he always tossed me pepperonis from the porch. They were delicious, but made me awfully thirsty. After a mouthful of pepperonis, I'd drink from the leaky faucet on the side of the house. I was down-right mad the day Clyde fixed it. Clyde was a pretty nice fella, but he tried to catch me once, and I just couldn't allow that. Eventually, he and Fluella moved away.

Tully's place always had good hotdogs and a warm fire to nap by. Tully tried to get me to come inside his camper. "Come in out of the cold," he offered.

Nah, I was fine outside.

Walking about became a daily routine for me. Sometimes I stayed near Panacea, but I often stretched my legs and ventured into Tallahassee, Woodville, and even Quincy. I'd slimmed down a bit, traveling from place to place.

I learned which people would feed me along my travels. Most of the people who worked at gas stations and restaurants always left something for me. It was disappointing when the people who I knew would feed me weren't home and other people would either shoo me away or just completely ignore me.

I was so hungry once that I stole a hotdog right off a stranger's grill while it was still cooking. The guy had stepped inside his camper for a minute, and I wasn't one to let an opportunity slip by. My front paws and tongue hurt for a week afterward, but it was worth it.

Some people even tried to catch me with traps. It always bothered me when I ran across a dog that was foolish enough to get himself captured in a trap. Shortly after I lost Jorene, I happened upon a puppy trapped in a wire cage near a dumpster. He howled pitifully. A few minutes later, two men arrived, picked up the cage with the puppy still in it, and loaded him up in their truck.

One of the men came back and replaced the puppy's cage with an empty one. I watched as he opened the door, propped it up, and carefully placed food in the far end of the cage. When he left, I checked it out. It didn't take me long to figure out that if I went in the cage, like the puppy, they'd find me howling too.

I wasn't as upset when I saw cats that had fallen for a trap. They were quickly taken away and I never saw them again. I was smart, smarter than most dogs, and definitely smarter than cats. Nope. I wasn't falling for a trap like that, no matter how good the food smelled.

I can only think of one time that I ate cat food. A horrible storm came up suddenly and I ran in a different direction than I normally do. It wasn't long before I was lost. Eventually, I came across a tiny house set back off the road. It was crawling with cats, but I was tired and hungry and soaking wet, so I decided to give it a try. When I whined at the screen door, a woman came out on the porch. She filled a bowl full of that nasty stuff and stood back beaming. I waited patiently for her to put something else, *anything* else, in the bowl, but she never did. I nibbled a few bites and left most of it for the ants.

If I wasn't in Panacea at my house with the mouse, I slept where ever I found a roof over my head: Old abandoned cars, under people's porches. When I was in Panacea, I visited the campground and sometimes a church. I often fell asleep listening to singing and music.

Surf Road was the route I traveled the most, unless it was firework season at the campground or a storm came through. The more miles between me and storms, the better.

One particular feeding spot, I enjoyed more than others. Down the road from the campground, on a side dirt road, nestled among pine trees that lined an old wooden fence, was where I met Russ. It wasn't by a house or a restaurant, so I'm not sure why he hung out there, but people do odd things sometimes.

I'd taken my usual short-cut down a dirt road, when I noticed an elderly looking man with white hair sitting on the tailgate of a Jeep. Nearby, two food bowls were piled high with food. That's all it took. When you find a good feeding place, you always come back.

Sometimes the man sat in his Jeep; other times, a lawn chair. Usually, I was already there in the shade of the woods nearby, watching and waiting for him.

After a few weeks of regular meals, he brought a bench to sit on instead of the lawn chair. A dome-like den with an opening appeared a few days later. It sat there for a few days before I investigated; dark and stuffy with a cobweb. I steered clear of it. How could you outrun a yellow fly, if one got in there with you? It could also be a trap.

We started a regular routine: He brought food and I ate it. His words tumbled out as easily as Jorene's. I didn't understand everything, but I listened as he dished out food. Once in a while, he even said my name.

"Here you go, boy. I gotcha another honey bun from the gas station." He peeled the wrapper back from the snack.

I didn't know his name for the longest time until a visitor rode by on a bike.

"Hey Russ, are you going to take him home today?"

"Nah, not yet, we're still getting to know each other. I'm in no rush, and I don't think he is either."

So, his name is Russ.

Hi Russ, I'm Honeybun.

"This fella's been around a while," the man with the bike said. He adjusted his bicycle helmet. "I've seen him for the last few years walking along the bike trail. People call him, 'that-yellow-dog'. I don't reckon I've ever heard anyone call him by a real name."

"Me either," Russ answered. He dropped another piece of honey bun in my bowl.

"Well, name him then. A dog can't go around in life without a name. Talk with you soon." The guy got back on his bike and off he rode.

Russ sat on the bench staring at me for a long while. He tilted his head to the right and scrunched his eyebrows. For a moment, I worried he was contemplating reaching out to touch me.

"Well, without a collar or tags, I have no idea if you're someone's pet taking advantage of everyone's generosity, or an actual stray," Russ said. "I'm guessing you were someone's pet at some time or other, because you ain't got the, *ahem*, marbles a stray from birth would have."

Russ scratched his head and jingled his keys. "I'd stay and chat some more, but I have errands to run. I'll be here tonight, so don't be late." He walked to his Jeep and left.

Russ was a pretty nice guy. Ever since Fluella left, no one else visited with me after they dropped off food. They either tossed it and moved on or tried to catch me. Russ was different. I liked Russ. Yep, I'd be back.

◊◊◊

True to his word, Russ pulled up in his Jeep that evening. I watched from the shade of the woods just past the tree line, out of sight of other people and dogs.

"Hey, Dude!" He yelled through cupped hands. "Got some chicken and dumplings!"

In my excitement, I couldn't slow down enough and trampled right on top of the bowl, spilling chicken and dumplings in the sand. It was still good and I ate it, grit and all, while Russ poured water in the other bowl.

"Slow down or you'll get a belly ache."

Russ didn't always make sense, but I wagged my tail to let him know I was happy. I don't wag my tail for just anyone.

After I ate, I rolled on my back in the sand. A yellow fly had gotten the better of me earlier and I couldn't get to the itch, but this helped. Russ squirted something on his arms and legs and rubbed it in. Yellow flies didn't seem to bother him like they did me. Occasionally he swatted at one, but for the most part, they hovered and passed him by.

He poured more water. "It's a hot day today. Drink up, you'll need it."

I slurped half of the water and sat about five feet away from him. We stared at each other.

"Sure wish you could talk. If you've been a stray as long as people say, you probably have a bunch of stories to share, don't you, ole Buddy?" He studied me. "Something tells me that you've experienced more than your average dog."

Russ talked about the campers down the road, and warned me that I should watch out for traffic when crossing the road as they weren't always looking for me. I listened intently to his advice.

"Gotta get home before supper's cold, but I'll be here in the morning." Russ pulled away in the Jeep and waved at me as he disappeared down Surf Road.

I trotted back to my house in the woods with a tummy full of warm food and pep in my step.

Chapter Ten

Early the next morning, several wild hogs rooted around outside my house, digging their snouts in the soil, searching for grub. If it was only one lonely pig, I might have barked and chased it away, but several of these fat, short-legged-animals were in the yard. Sharp tusks jutted forward from the sides of their mouths. I stayed as quiet as possible, watching them from the window.

After several minutes, I gingerly stepped off the porch, avoiding confrontation, and started toward the campground to get fed, but dogs bayed in the distance. The hogs scattered in different directions. I stood there, judging the distance of the dogs, when voices of men mingled with the baying. I dashed back inside and watched through the window as several men and dogs emerged from the woods. The men held tight to the dogs by leashes.

"They ran through this area, Lemuel," one man called out, "See, here, right here! These are tracks."

The other men went in opposite directions with their dogs' noses to the ground, stirring up leaves, confused by the scents of multiple trails.

"I don't think those are hog tracks. Looks more like dog tracks."

"I believe *these* are dog tracks." He stepped to the right, knelt down and touched the disturbed leaves on the ground. "But these are *hog* tracks."

Their dogs looked like the ones I'd seen in cages in the back of pickup trucks: Taller and leaner than me, short haired, mostly white, with brown and black spots all over. I knew I was right to stay out of those cages; first the cage, then a leash.

The dogs kept their faces to the ground and zigzagged as they followed the various scents. One second they were on the hog tracks, next they smelled where I peed against the tree last night. Then back onto the hog tracks. One of them pulled its owner up to the steps of my house.

"Trigger, this way." The young man jerked his dog back, but Trigger ignored him and pulled harder toward the steps.

Not even a split second passed and the dog bayed, charging the door, making the other dogs react. They busted through the door, pulling their owners as they struggled to hold onto their leashes.

I ran out the back door and was half-way across the yard, before one of the men shouted. "It's a dog, Trigger, Stop! It's just a feral dog."

Their baying faded in the background as I dodged through the pine trees, jumped over small bushes, and scared a foraging squirrel up a tree. I paused at a small creek, drank, and caught my breath.

A snort alerted me. Three hogs spotted me and charged. I tried to nip one when it got too close, and narrowly missed getting jabbed by tusks. I ran through the creek to escape them.

That was a first for me; running from people, dogs, and hogs all at the same time. With my unexpected company this morning, I didn't get a chance to visit with Russ, and I was hungry. I resorted to digging through a trash can near a trailer in the woods.

It wasn't Tully's trash or I would have simply scratched on his door. This family didn't like me, but their teenage son never put the trashcan lid on right and it was easy to knock off. I tried many times to get to know the woman in the house, but anytime I got near her, she sneezed and shooed me away. Usually, I waited until late at night when they were asleep to raid their trash, but this time I was bold, and it paid off.

I had a long walk on a full stomach to the campground, but I made it. Russ was nowhere in sight. I stayed in the woods just past the tree line with a perfect view of his bench, so I knew I wouldn't miss him coming. I enjoyed a long nap and only a couple mosquitoes bothered me.

A horn beeped, waking me instantly. Russ stood over my bowl, holding a bag, and looking around. "Come on, boy," he yelled.

I stretched and walked across the field to say hey.

"Well, I'm glad you could make it," Russ said with a funny tone. "I was here this morning, fighting with the yellow flies, just to bring you sausage and grits. Were you here? No."

I wagged my tail, waiting to see what he would put in the bowl.

"I have ground pork and baked beans. I'm thinking you won't eat the baked beans, but you've been eating everything lately, so, better you than the trashcan."

I gobbled it down and tasted something dry and powdery in the last bite. I tried to separate it from the good stuff in the food, but I couldn't, so I swallowed it all.

"Good boy. Hopefully that pill will keep the fleas and ticks off of you. I saw you scratching the other day, when you rolled around on the grass. Either you were very happy or had an itch."

Russ sat on the bench and brought out another package. "I brought a honey bun."

My head perked up at the sound of my name. I trotted over to him.

Russ pinched off five pieces and laid them in a line on the bench. I waited until he was done and ate the three pieces that were farthest from where Russ sat.

I drank water he left in the bowl, hoping it would get rid of the funny taste in my mouth. It almost did, almost.

"There's a storm coming, Dude. I hope you have shelter."

Russ chatted a little longer, but stopped when I trotted off. I didn't mean to be rude; it's just that I got a whiff of something at the campground and wanted to check it out.

"You can't burn plastic; you know that, Ned," a woman fussed, pulling a long strip of plastic from a bonfire. "We'll get kicked out of the campground,"

They argued and didn't notice me inching closer to watch them. A piece of hotdog rolled off Ned's dinner plate while they argued and laid resting on his bare foot. I slowly stepped over, trying to get close enough to retrieve that tempting morsel.

"If you'd thrown it away like I asked last night, I wouldn't have been tryin' to burn it." His voice was gruff with anger. I crept closer.

The woman carried the plastic strip on the end of a long stick to the dumpster. She tossed it in, stick and all. She was still angry. "I like it here. Don't mess this up for me." She stormed off to their camper and slammed the door.

My teeth were almost around the hotdog when the smell of the plastic tickled my nose hairs and I sneezed on the man's bare feet. He looked down at me and said, "This would be a good time for you to run."

Now I don't understand all of what humans say, but the look on his face was very clear. I ran right straight out of the campground and back to where Russ had been, but he wasn't there anymore.

I ate the last two pieces of the honey bun he had left on the bench and crawled underneath to lick between the boards for the last bit of sweetness that had dripped between them. I laid there for a while, shaded from the sun, watching the cars go by. A few people rode their bikes and looked my way. One guy waved and yelled at me, "Hey, Surf Dude."

I'd heard the word *Dude* more often lately, especially when Russ talked to me. It's sure different than Honeybun, but I liked it.

A warm breeze blew across my face, ruffling my fur. I almost didn't see the black and white cat that walked up to check out the food bowl. I don't think it saw me either.

I've always had a dislike for cats. Especially since a yellow one swiped my face a few years ago and nicked my nose. I chased it across a vacant lot and through a pasture full of grazing cows. It darted between their legs and scrambled up a tree. By the time I left, cows had gathered around the tree again, sheltering from the hot sun. I'm pretty sure the cat might still be up in that tree.

But this was a different cat entirely. This cat was fearless, sticking its face where it didn't belong: my bowl. I darted out from under the bench and charged. That cat did a back flip, knocked my bowl over, and climbed up a tree faster than I could run in a straight line. I didn't even get a chance to chase it, which I love to do. I sat on the ground beneath the tree, looked up and growled. The cat climbed higher, almost hidden in the branches. I woofed once for good measure, walked back to the bench, crawled under it, and took another nap.

When I woke up, the sun was starting to go down and Russ was just driving up.

"Hey, Dude, this is a change. You're here before me. You been waiting long?" He unpacked my food and poured it in the bowl. He talked for a while about nothing important. One of his friends stopped by and brought some steak he'd cooked. Russ took a few bites and dropped the rest in my bowl.

Russ was saying goodbye and the cat meowed. I'd almost forgotten about the cat. Russ looked up in the tree and back at me.

"Is there something I need to know?"

I wagged my tail.

"I'm learning new things about you every day," Russ said with a chuckle. "You have two things you don't like: cats and being touched."

Russ climbed in his Jeep and rolled down the window. "Let me tell you something that I don't like: dogs that are late for breakfast. Don't be late tomorrow."

I walked to the wooded area across the field and looked back to see the cat climbing down from the tree butt first. I thought of waiting until it was in the middle of the field and chasing it, but I figured it had learned its lesson.

Chapter Eleven

It's funny the things a stray dog learns along the way. My sense of danger was keener than dogs that have owners. Maybe that was because it was just me and I knew I had to take care of myself. I learned where to find shelter, food, and water; all the things I needed to survive.

For a few days, I didn't go the campground because a storm came through. By the time it passed, I was starved. I hoped I hadn't missed Russ. He always came twice a day, in the morning and in the evening.

Another car pulled up into the spot where Russ usually parked. A woman I'd never seen before got out of the car carrying a small bag. She looked around and yelled the same name that Russ did when he called me, but I didn't budge. The woman dropped something in the bowl, called a few more times, and sat on the bench waiting, but I was a no-show. After she drove away, I trotted over to see what she brought.

It overflowed the bowl and smelled weird. I'd never eaten this before, but gave it a try. I was sitting by the bowl, still licking grease from my lips, when Russ pulled up.

"Hey, Dude! Where have you been?" He stepped out of his Jeep. "I've been by each day, like clock-work, with food, but haven't seen you. I've had shrimp, hushpuppies, steak, ground beef, and all sorts of good food." Russ smiled and filled my bowl. "I have some more shrimp and hushpuppies today. Eat up." Russ sat on the bench and read his newspaper.

I walked over to the bowl, sniffed it, and sat down to look at him.

"Not interested? Dude, this is good stuff," he encouraged.

I pulled a shrimp out with my teeth, dug a shallow hole with one paw, dropped the shrimp in the hole, and covered it up with the same paw.

"Are you kidding me? I've heard of dogs that bury bones, but a dog that buries shrimp?" Russ shook his head and slapped his newspaper down on the bench. "I've been out here every day, twice a day, for the past five days looking for you. Today I bring you shrimp and hushpuppies, and you bury them in the dirt."

He shook his head again. "I've had dogs my whole life growing up, but you have got to be the rudest mutt of them all. And to think, I do all this and you won't even let me pet you. It's a full-time job taking care of you with no benefits."

I looked at Russ, cocked my head sideways, and woofed at him.

"Yeah, yeah, I know. I'll be here tomorrow."

◊◊◊

When I got home, my front door was wide open. It was never wide open. Voices, *two* voices came from inside my house. I stepped closer.

"Tucker, this place is cool. This could be our fort."

"Maybe, but it smells funny. Something probably crawled up in that couch and died."

The other voice answered. "Who cares? It's still cool."

I placed my paws on the windowsill, careful to avoid the broken glass, and looked in. Two boys walked around, poking at things that didn't belong to them. They even moved the couch cushions and coat around, after I'd finally gotten them squished down so the spring didn't poke me anymore. This was my house!

"We could always pull the couch outside far away. That might take care of the smell."

"You get one end and I'll get the other."

As they dragged my couch across the floor to the front door, the white mouse jumped out of it, unnoticed, and scurried across the floor. It hid beneath old newspapers in the corner of the living room.

This had to stop. That was my couch they were moving, my house they were trespassing in, and my mouse they scared. I stepped in the doorway and showed myself.

"Dewey, the, the, there's a wolf behind you," Tucker whispered, not taking his eyes off me.

Tucker whipped around. He stood a couple inches taller than Dewey, but they were both young kids. Not even teenagers. They looked terrified, even though all I did was stand there watching them.

"Daddy said that there were rabid animals in the woods, and that we shouldn't leave the property without him," Dewey said. "I thought he was teasing, just to keep us at the house and out of trouble."

Beads of sweat popped up on Tucker's forehead and a new smell tickled my nose. I knew that smell. It was fear. It mingled with the same smell that came from Dewey. I didn't mean to scare them *that* bad. I just wanted them out of my house. I had a change of heart and stepped forward, trying to be nice.

Dewey, the smaller boy, gasped. "Tucker, is that foam around his mouth?" His voice was higher pitched than before.

Tucker stammered, "M-maybe this fort wasn't such a great idea."

Tucker and Dewey slowly lowered the couch. Whew, glad they weren't going to take it. It smelled just fine to me.

Tucker pulled a cloth from his pocket and wiped sweat from his forehead. He didn't notice the half-eaten packet of crackers that fell from his pocket to the floor. The mouse saw the chance for a snack and ran to the crackers. I yipped at him to stay hidden.

Dewey's high-pitched squeal hurt my ears, and I barked at him to stop. Tucker grabbed Dewey by the shirt collar and dragged him across the couch, almost pulling his shirt off of him in the process. Both of them ran to the back of the house and jumped out a broken window.

Dewey's shoe stayed behind, dangling by the shoestring on the broken glass. I grabbed it in my mouth and tried to take it to them, but the closer I got, the faster they ran. I gave up and left it several yards in the woods. Maybe they'd come back and get it.

It took a while for me to push the couch back across the floor to where it belonged, shoving it with my shoulder. I never got it back in the original spot, but it was close enough.

A few minutes later the mouse came back too. I named my room-mate Marvin. I figured Marvin and I'd been through a lot recently, and he deserved a name too.

Dewey and Tucker never visited again.

◊◊◊

I made a point of being at the feeding spot the next morning before Russ arrived. Someone had put what looked like dry dog food in the bowl. I pushed the brown nuggets around with my nose until the bowl tipped over and the dog food fell out. Russ would need a clean bowl to put the good stuff in. Three people walked by with hyper dogs, and two cars almost crashed taking pictures of me before Russ pulled up.

"Hey Dude, sorry I'm late. I had errands to run. Have I got something good for you!" Russ pulled a container out of a bag and plopped a huge bone with big chunks of meat dangling from it into my bowl. "You better not have eaten elsewhere this morning."

Drool pooled in my jowls and slipped down in a string. Russ backed up and I checked out the food more closely.

"Yeah, I thought you'd go for this."

A couple of ants discovered the dog food that I had knocked out of the bowl. Russ scooped up the pellets and tossed them over the fence. "Smart choice."

You too, Russ, I thought.

I laid down in front of the bowl, gnawing on the bone, and watched Russ pull more items from the bag. I had no idea what could be better than this bone, but I was interested to see if Russ knew of something. I held the bone in my mouth, waiting.

"We had friends over the other night and we still had burgers leftover. I always think of you, Dude. Don't forget that."

Russ sat down on the bench and brought a honey bun out of the bag. "This is dessert," he said with a big smile.

I dropped the bone right beside the food bowl and ate while Russ read his newspaper. I finished what was in the bowl, picked up my bone, and started to leave.

"Hey, don't forget your honey bun."

I stopped, turned around, and looked at Russ. He held out a piece of the honey bun for me to take from his hand.

Russ knew better, but he always tried.

I contemplated which would be better; the bone or the honey bun. I laid down to think about it and fell asleep with the bone in my mouth.

I'm not sure how long I napped, but Russ woke me up when he got off the bench. I trotted over to claim my honey bun.

"Sorry, Dude. I ate it." Russ licked his fingers. "Never hesitate when it comes to honey buns."

I buried my bone for later and went home.

Chapter Twelve

Russ and I became a team. I depended on him to bring me food in the morning and evening, and he depended on me to have an appetite. And most of the time I did. I couldn't help it if people set off fireworks, or if a thunderstorm came around. I can't be around for that. He wasn't always happy when I showed up days later with a full stomach, but at least I showed up.

I trotted up to the feeding place one morning with a good appetite, ready to eat. Russ hammered on the fence above my dog bowl. I waited until he stopped before walking to him.

"It's about time you showed up. I thought you'd found someone else to love."

I sniffed at the food in the bowl. Russ hammered in the last nail and I jumped. "Okay, I'll wait until you're gone. Maybe this will stop people from feeding you. I know you can't read, Dude, so I'll read it to you. PLEASE DON'T FEED THIS DOG. HE NEEDS TO BE HUNGRY TO TAKE HIS MEDICINE. THANK YOU."

Russ tossed me a piece of a hotdog and I caught it midair. "With everyone feeding you, I can't give you heartworm and flea medicine on schedule. When you're hungry, you eat so fast you don't even realize you've eaten your meds too."

Russ looked at the sign. "This ain't gonna work is it, Dude? People have a hard time doing what a stop sign says. Who am I to think they'll pay attention to this?"

Russ pulled a thin, rectangular object from his pocket and held it to his ear. "What did you say again? I can't hear you. Are you on Spring Hill? The connection is bad on that road." He paused for a moment. "Okay."

Russ looked at me. "Daniel said to tell you hey."

Then he spoke into the object again. "All right, I'll get pictures of Surf Dude."

Russ held the rectangular object up for me to look at. "Hey, Dude, say 'honey bun.'"

The object clicked and Russ looked at it. "That's a good one. I don't know if I've told you, but someone started a social media page about you. You're becoming a local celebrity. Even the out-of-towners are learning about you. Everyone gets excited when they spot you walking the streets. It's like spotting Bigfoot, but you're seen more often."

I dug up an old bone and chewed on the end for a while as Russ talked about the weather and who was coming over for supper later.

"You could come home and have supper with us. Just jump up in this Jeep here," Russ coaxed.

Not happening, Russ, but thanks for the offer, I thought. I tried to dig a hole deep enough to rebury the entire bone, but the end of it stuck up. Oh well, it'd be easier to find again. I trotted off down the street.

"You're welcome," Russ yelled.

I looked over my shoulder and wagged my tail a few times as a thank you.

Russ was the one constant that I could depend on, even if he couldn't depend on me. I was surprised when he missed a few days, but a couple ladies dropped by to visit me and left food. I learned their names were Rae and Nina, and they left the same type of food Russ did.

I liked listening to them talk and always stayed around longer when they came by. They had soft voices like Jorene. But I missed Russ.

◊◊◊

One morning, while waiting for Russ to bring me food, I tried to catch a Georgia Thumper that was annoying me. I almost had it when Russ pulled up and yelled for me. Still frustrated that he didn't tell me about his change in plans, namely that he was sending someone else to feed me, I decided to make him wait for me for a change.

He walked around calling my name. He looked in the direction of the campground, walked to the sidewalk, looked to the left and then the right and called again. Finally, he sat on the tailgate and opened his newspaper. I stayed right where I was and watched him. I didn't mean to fall asleep, but woke when I heard the Jeep crank. Russ's Jeep came to an abrupt stop when I ran in front of it and stopped. We stared at each other through the front windshield. Now that I had his attention, I trotted over to the feeding place and sat down by my bowl.

He rolled down his window. "The food's cold now."

I pranced around the bowl and whined.

He pulled back down the dirt road and parked a few feet from the bench.

"You're a mess, you know that?"

I spun around in excitement while he mixed up the food.

"All right, all right, settle down." He set the bowl at my feet and I ate until I heard something crinkle. Russ removed the wrapping from a honey bun, broke it in pieces, and placed them on his tailgate. I walked over to check and put my front paws, one by one, on the tailgate for balance. I kept one eye on the honey bun pieces and one eye on Russ, just in case this was a trick, and ate a few pieces.

"Hey Russ," a man shouted from the road. It was one of Russ's friends taking his dog for a walk. The large black dog's pointy ears perked up when it saw me, and it wagged its nub of a tail. Its interest in me faded when it sat down and scratched behind its ear. I on the other hand, was fully alert and stood in front of Russ's Jeep, protecting Russ and my honey bun. I didn't growl as I didn't want to start anything, but ain't anybody taking my honey bun.

"Looks like Surf Dude isn't too fond of Barney, here," the man said. Barney sniffed the ground, and completely ignored me.

Russ lowered his newspaper. "Come to think of it, I've never seen Dude around another dog. He's peculiar like that."

"I'll catch you later, Russ."

I peed on the ground behind Russ's Jeep, kicked up some dirt with my back legs, and strutted back to Russ. The last piece of the honey bun went down with one gulp. I rolled in the sand to scratch an itch and then headed in the same direction as the guy and his dog.

"The tailgate is always down, Dude, just in case you change your mind."

I kept walking.

◊◊◊

I caught up with the guy with the dog and followed at a safe distance. I couldn't figure out why dogs allowed themselves to be lead around like that. I crossed over the highway before the bridge and kept going. The man and his dog disappeared into a house, and I decided to walk a bit more.

I'd been on this side of the road many times over the years and it pretty much looked like the other side, except there was more marshlands and a large creek that went under the road near a place where people put their boats in the water.

I sniffed a dead possum on the side of the road that the buzzards hadn't found yet. The palmetto bushes across the road parted a bit and a long snout poked out, with sharp teeth that jutted up and down. The sharp blades of the palmetto didn't even bother it. I'd never seen anything like it; mottled brown in color, with bumps on its back and head. Dogs know on instinct if something is to be feared, and I felt a little nervous. It smelled like something rotten. For the first time in my life, I wasn't sure what to do. This creature was scarier than the bear encounter. It opened its mouth and hissed. A car pulled up between us. I lowered my head and watched the beast under the car.

"Irma, that's Surf Dude having a standoff with a gator," the lady driver yelled at her friend in the passenger seat.

"Stop yelling in my ear, Carla, I'm right here! Honk the horn, that'll scare it."

Carla rolled down her window and waved her hand at the gator as if shooing away a fly.

"Get, you ugly old gator! You mess with Surf Dude and you'll have a mob after you."

The gator stood as still as the blue water tower by my feeding place.

"We can't let it get Surf Dude. Get out and scare the gator away," Carla ordered Irma.

Irma's eyes became huge. "Have you lost your mind? I ain't getting out of this car."

"You have to do something," Carla begged. "If people knew we were here and didn't save him, we'd have to join the witness relocation program, and I'm one of Surf Dude's biggest followers."

"Well, he does have fans in Ireland," Irma said.

"Always the drama queen, aren't you? Do something before we're late for Bingo."

Carla revved the car's engine and honked the horn a couple more times. The gator hissed at them.

"Here," Irma moved about in the car. "I found a half-eaten burger in this bag from Craven's country store. I can throw it one way and maybe Surf will run the other while the gator goes for the burger."

Carla frowned. "We went to Craven's five days ago. You mean to tell me you left that in my car this whole time? I thought I smelled something. You beat everything, you know that?" Carla rolled her eyes and Irma held the leftover burger out the window.

"Here gator, gator, gator," Carla sang in a high-pitched voice that made my ears perk up. "Fetch!" She tossed the bag out the window toward the rear of the car. It tumbled in the dirt.

I almost went for the bag without thinking. I saw the gator from under the belly of the car move in the direction of the burger.

Irma and Carla leaned over out Irma's window. "Run, Surf! Run," they yelled in unison. I wasn't sure exactly what they were trying to do, but I ran in the opposite direction of the gator.

I lost my balance and fell into the palmetto bushes. Disoriented and trying to get away from the gator and the car, I tore through the bushes. Spiky leaves scraped my sides, but I didn't slow down until my feet splashed in water.

A large creek stretched ahead. I was able to walk through some parts, but the water was over my head most of the way, and I swam. Three white birds with long black legs perched on a fallen tree, clinging to it with their bright yellow feet. Two of them watched me with suspicious eyes, while the third was preoccupied with a fish flapping desperately from his slender black beak. The one with the fish in his beak took flight, skimming within inches of the top of my head. I swallowed nasty marsh water trying to get to the other shore.

I scrambled up the embankment. With a solid surface beneath my feet, I ran hard on the back road and wore part of the padding off my back feet. I didn't stop until I was back at the campground across from the feeding spot. I stopped long enough to drink some water from a leaky spigot at the campground, and hobbled all the way to the house in the woods. I didn't even check to see if Russ was waiting at the feeding place.

I took a shortcut that went through a neighborhood. That's where I saw something that shook me to my core. It was Herman, an old bloodhound that I'd meet a few years back. Neither one of us had ever been friendly to each other, but as a courtesy, I didn't chase him when his owner walked him on a leash.

It wasn't Herman that caught me by surprise, but rather the small grey kitten that snuggled up against him, sleeping soundly against his belly.

Herman saw me, stood up, and howled. The kitten raised its head, jumped up, and hissed at me.

I was exhausted; I wouldn't even have the energy to chase Marvin if I wanted to, much less mess with Herman and that kitten. Herman and I had never officially met each other as his owner usually jerked him away from me when he saw me coming, but I'd have to explain to Herman what was acceptable and what was not when it came to dog/cat relationships.

When I reached my house, I was too tired to stand on three legs to pee, so I squatted near a bush in front of the house. I was glad no-one was around to see my humiliating act.

I limped up the stairs and crawled onto the couch. Marvin popped out from underneath one of the cushions to check on me. Satisfied that I was home to keep him company, he scurried back under the cushion. I turned around three times to the left, once to the right, and fell over on the cushion. I licked my sore paws until I fell asleep.

Chapter Thirteen

I met Russ at our feeding place the next morning. The area was a mess. My food bowl was several yards away and turned upside down. The towel that Russ kept in the doghouse rested on the other side of the fence. The ground reeked of another animal.

"You didn't do this, did you Dude?" Russ fussed. "Or maybe you were getting even because I've been late a few times?" He picked up my bowl and wiped it clean with a wet cloth. "I came by last night and waited a while. I had all your favorites: pizza, home fries, and chicken and dumplings." He poured last night's leftovers into the bowl. "There might even be a hushpuppy in here for you."

I nosed around the pizza and nibbled on the fries. I had hoped he would bring shrimp and grits, but I guess this food was okay.

"You're looking a little bit sluggish there. Are you getting fed better somewhere else? What's eating you? Don't you like dumplings anymore? I remember a time when you were excited to get dog food, but now I think this celebrity thing has gone to your head and you're too good for dog food now."

I pushed the food around, ate two more fries, and stopped.

"It's this or I start bringing dog food again, what's it going to be?"

If he only knew that yesterday was crazy: I was almost a meal for a gator, swam in a creek until exhausted, ran until my paws nearly bled, squatted to pee, and the worst thing of all was seeing a cat and dog snuggle. I know I live with a mouse, but that's different.

Give me a break, Russ. I picked out a hushpuppy and buried it at the woods for later. Russ covered the food bowl, but I came back for more.

"Well excuse me. Hasn't anyone ever told you not to leave the table unless you're done? I thought you were leaving."

I ignored him as I ate more.

"My mother would have liked you. She always liked a man that cleaned his plate." Russ picked up my bowl, cleaned it, and put it just inside the domed dog house that I refused to step inside of. "Seeing as how we have this very expensive food pantry, I'm going to store your food in here. I think the buzzards must have messed it up yesterday. Maybe they won't see it from above. I'll be back this evening around 7ish. Don't be late or you'll get dog food." He got in his Jeep and left.

◊◊◊

I laid by the dog house for a bit, watching traffic drive by until I fell asleep with the sun on my face. When the sun was above my head, I strolled over to the campground and slept under a picnic table. It was the perfect spot to rest my feet and catch dropped scraps at the same time.

The kids in the campground didn't bother me and I was happy to be left alone. Occasionally, the click of a camera would wake me up, but I was too tired to care. As long as food kept falling from above, I was content to stay here.

Dark clouds blew across the sky, darkening the campground. I hoped Russ wouldn't be late tonight. I walked across the road and waited. I pulled my bowl from inside the doghouse and placed it in front of my paws just as Russ pulled up.

"Ah, you're on time. Guess you didn't want dog food, huh?" He filled the bowl. "I brought a few very well-endowed chicken-breasts for you to enjoy. Eat up."

I cleaned the bowl better than ants would have.

"Word around town is that you met a gator down the road." Russ sat on the bench and pulled out a honey bun. "I've seen a few gators basking in the sun on the side of the roads lately."

A muffled tune came from Russ's pants pocket. "That would be my phone," he said as he pulled out the little rectangular object I'd seen him use before. Russ talked into his phone and pointed it at me. "Your fans need an update. Smile." The phone clicked several times.

"The weatherman said there's a hurricane coming our way. I sure wish you'd let me take you home."

I turned to Russ and yawned.

"I know, I know. I need to stop nagging."

Russ read his newspaper while I enjoyed a nap in the warm grass with a full belly. I didn't wake up until a car pulled up and parked beside Russ's Jeep. A short, pudgy man stepped out and waddled over to Russ.

"Hey, how's Surf Dude doing?"

Russ chuckled. "He's a spoiled rotten dog. It wouldn't surprise me if he gets his own reality show."

"I wouldn't expect anything else. Get home before the hurricane hits. It's gonna be a bad one."

"Thanks, Pete. I'm heading out in a minute." Russ folded up his newspaper and Pete drove away.

"If you ain't coming home with me, you better get to wherever it is you get to when it rains, because we got a good one coming tonight." Russ opened the door to his Jeep and patted the seat, encouraging me to jump in.

I didn't budge.

"Just as I thought. I'll drop by tomorrow if the weather permits." Russ slid into the driver's seat and left.

Wind gusts picked up and the air smelled sweet and pungent, like wet earth getting kicked up. I made one last round at the campground, checking out grills for leftovers or anything that had been left behind. Only two campers remained. They packed their belongings quickly and tossed leftovers to me as they left. I buried the food scraps in the dirt for later.

The first sprinkles before the storm dropped on my head and I raced home. As I reached the porch, a small branch from the tree closest to the house fell to the ground with a thump. The wind had picked up and a few leaves had gathered against the outside wall of the porch; even more had been blown in the house through the open door and broken window.

I curled up on the couch to wait out the storm. Marvin made an appearance, but a flash of lightning crackled and he dove under the cushion. We would both be dry tonight. I slept for a bit, until the thunder rumbled so loud, I thought the floor boards had rattled loose. Water leaked through the roof in a few spots, leaving small puddles on the floor. Lightning flashed again and Marvin scurried to another room. Rain poured down like a thick wall of gray, making the trees outside the window barely visible. The sound of branches battering the roof kept me awake.

I couldn't go outside, and I knew better than to pee inside. I tried to wait until the rain stopped, but the longer I waited the harder it poured. I couldn't hold it any longer. I peed right at the foot of the porch steps. Rain fell sideways, stinging my face.

I ran back inside and shook, spraying water across the floor. I rubbed my face and body against the couch to dry off more. I curled back up on the couch, closed my eyes against the storm, and shivered.

I ventured outside the next morning, but it was raining too hard for me to meet Russ. I was starving and paced, deciding what to do. Tully lived closer and always has something for me to eat. I ran through the woods to Tully's and by the time I arrived, I was wet as a fish.

I scratched at his door and it creaked open. Lightning cracked and I boldly took two steps inside. I barked to let him know I was there; still no Tully.

I crept through the trailer, but no one was there. It was warm and dry. The roof didn't leak, either.

Three partially covered containers of food sat on the counter. I knew I shouldn't, but I put my paws on the counter and nudged the covering off the top of one. It was chicken! I tried to only take one piece, but the entire container fell on the floor. I ate as much as I could so it wouldn't be a mess when Tully came home. I wondered what was in the other container and pushed off its covering. Potatoes mixed with something. I ate some of it.

I turned to leave, but rain came down even harder now. I'd never been inside someone's house without being invited. Tully's bed and white blanket were softer than the coat I slept on at the abandoned house, and he even had feather pillows like

Jorene's. I curled up between the pillows and took a nap, waiting for the rain to stop.

◊◊◊

I woke up when I heard a truck door slam. Tully was home! I ran to the door to escape before he came in, but the wind had blown the front door closed. I was trapped in his house. I hid behind the couch.

Apparently, I didn't clean up the floor as good as I thought. He stepped on the paper that had covered the chicken and stomped into the kitchen.

"What the hell. Who's here?" He didn't see me and I slipped farther behind the couch, wishing I was invisible.

After he passed the couch, there was nothing between me and the open door. I jumped over the back of the couch, scaring him so bad he fell backward in front of the open door. I landed on his chest, bounced right off him, and out the door into the rain. I'd rather get soaked than caught.

"I hope you enjoyed the chicken and potatoes!" he yelled.

It would be a while before I visited him again.

Chapter Fourteen

I curled up in a tight ball on my couch and didn't move for a long time. It rained off and on for the rest of the day, finally dissipating to a drizzle.

I rushed to the feeding place, hoping to see Russ. He wasn't there. I looked at the dog house. Maybe I should try it out while I waited for him to show up with food. Each time I heard an automobile I stuck my head out, expecting Russ's Jeep, but it wasn't.

Finally, I gave up. I ran for the restaurant, but they were closed and had boards across their windows.

Next, I checked out the corner gas station. The trash can had chicken wings right on top. I didn't even have to dig for them. I was eating the last wing when a piece of the gas station roof fell off, barely missing me. I yipped, tucked my tail between my legs, and ran with the wing clamped in my mouth.

Big branches and even entire trees laid on the ground, scattered in the roads and culverts. A boat that should have been in the water rested on dry land, leaning against a building. The buzz of chainsaws filled the air and an ambulance whizzed by with the siren wailing.

I traveled farther into Tallahassee to get food and spent a few days there. The day I discovered airplanes was also the day that I busted my nose. When you hear a roar from above and look up to see an enormous white bird-like creature with wings coming down fast, you run. I ran right into the chain-link fence, face first. My nose hurt for a week after that. I watched those big birds take off and land for a few days. They made a lot of noise but were harmless.

I missed home and decided to see if Russ was waiting at the feeding place.

My bowls were half way down the dirt road and the doghouse had been blown on its side. There was no Russ. I turned to go and was almost in the woods, when the familiar sound of his Jeep made me jump with excitement. I'd never been so happy to see Russ. I ran and barked at the same time. I tripped on my own feet, tumbled over my head, and got back on my feet, running full speed to Russ. I misjudged how close I was to the bowl and couldn't stop. I trampled over it, spilling all the food that he'd just poured.

"Just a little hungry there, aren't you?"

I gobbled up the food on the ground.

Russ refilled my bowl. I didn't even wait for him to move his hands before I shoved my mouth in the bowl.

"Easy there, Dude," Russ said, checking out his hand and counting fingers.

"You're looking a little slim." He let the tailgate down and sat on it. "That hurricane was something else, wasn't it? We lost a few shingles off our roof. Good thing I bought that generator last year."

I licked the bowl clean. I gazed at Russ, licking my chops.

"You want more?" He pulled a bag out of his Jeep. When he opened it, I smelled ham.

"People have been saying that you've been coming by here, but it's not at our usual feeding time. Sorry I kept missing you, but I was checking."

He dropped big juicy chunks of ham in the bowl. They had a sweet coating on top, but I didn't care. I ate so fast, I almost choked on one piece. Russ looked concerned when he saw me hawking, but I got it up and back down again. Russ sat back down on his tailgate.

"Remember that social media page I told you about a while back? Well, lots more people are following you. You have fans from as far away as California. I think you even have someone in Ireland. Can you believe that?"

I yawned and flicked my ear to get a yellow fly to leave me alone. It bit my rear and I jumped.

"Ah, you're excited about having a fan in Ireland, eh? I've been writing about our conversations," Russ chuckled. "I guess it's more one-sided conversations. You have quite a fan base here, Dude. Everyone was worried about you during that hurricane."

Russ dropped a few more chunks of meat in my bowl and pulled out a second bag with a honey bun in it. I ate the meat while he unwrapped my dessert.

"People asked if you were living with me. I had to tell them that you don't trust me like that, yet. Sure do wish I knew where you stayed when the weather turns bad. You better not have an owner and kids to play with and been inside sleeping on a nice soft dog bed, while I'm out here getting' up at the crack of dawn, in a hurricane, to bring you food."

Russ pinched off a piece of the honey bun and tossed it to me.

"I get text messages all the time from people telling me that they've seen you. Some of them, I'm not sure if I believe. There

85

are reports of you all the way up near Quincy. For the life of me, I just can't see you going that far."

He pinched off another piece of my dessert and ate it himself. I wasn't even hungry anymore, but I kept an eye on it.

"You want more?" He reached in the bag and tore off another piece, placing it on the tailgate. He rested the half-empty bag on his leg.

I was already full, but walked over to give it a sniff. I took the morsel off the tailgate and ate it. I don't know what possessed me, but I snatched the bag, turned, and ran before Russ could stop me.

"Didn't your mama teach you about sharing?" I heard him yell as I disappeared into the woods.

◊◊◊

I dropped the honey bun on the couch and waited for Marvin. His nose made an appearance first, pushing up between two cushions. I nudged the bag closer to Marvin. Marvin scooted out and crawled inside the bag to nibble on the honey bun. Marvin was stuck here, and I had to take care of my buddy.

Chapter Fifteen

Since I moved to Florida, I've seen a lot of different kinds of animals: some swim, fly, slither, or hop. But the day I heard clucking, I stopped in my tracks. Usually I ran so fast that the only thing I heard were my feet pounding the ground. On this particular morning, I wasn't in a hurry because Russ had brought me a huge meal the night before. The noise came from the front of a house that faced the beach.

Curiosity could be a bad thing; I'd already learned that a few times. But maybe this time, it would be different. I trotted around the side of the house to investigate.

I'd seen birds before: seagulls, pelicans, cranes, and birds smaller than Marvin, but nothing prepared me for this. These birds were chubby, with short little beaks and stubby legs. They strutted around in a fenced area. A young girl tossed a few small tomatoes into the pen. The birds clucked louder, trampled on top of each other, flapping their wings, and pecked at the ground in excitement.

"Paisley, hurry up and feed the chickens," a voice called from the house. "We have to go."

I laid down and watched to learn more about these short-legged birds. I crept closer, hoping to stay hidden, but the chickens saw me and clucked louder. The little girl jumped.

"Hi, I'm Paisley." She tossed me a small tomato. I sniffed it but wasn't interested. "What's your name? Do you live around here?"

Paisley didn't try to pet me or chase me like other kids did. She spoke softly and I liked her instantly.

"You're pretty," she said, and I wagged my tail. "Don't leave. I'll be right back." She disappeared into her house. I stepped closer to the chickens and they flapped their wings. White feathers flew everywhere. I was about to leave when Paisley came back out.

"Here," she tossed me a couple cookies. "Butterball made them."

I swallowed them in one gulp.

The back door opened and a woman stood in the doorway.

"Well lookie there, Paisley, you know who that is? That's Surf Dude. He's a celebrity in this town."

Paisley leaned close to me. "That's Butterball. Don't tell her I gave you cookies."

"Too late, I already saw you," Butterball stated. "How many did you give him?"

Paisley held up two fingers.

"That's enough. I follow Surf Dude on his social media page and he has people feeding him on a regular schedule. If you give him more than that, he might not show up at feeding time. Mr. Russ needs to make sure he's hungry to get his monthly meds."

Paisley rolled her eyes, "Yes, Ma'am."

I licked my lips, still watching the chickens. Butterball stepped in the yard, glared at me, and frowned. She went inside, but came back with half a dozen cookies. She tossed them at my feet.

"Hey, I thought you said no more cookies." Paisley stood with her hands on her hips.

"He's too interested in my chickens. I'm making sure he leaves here with a full belly, but not with one of those chickens. I'll apologize to Russ later."

◊◊◊

One of my stops was a faded yellow house half-way between Panacea and Sopchoppy where I visited a teenage boy. A huge sprawling oak tree in the front yard had squirrel feeders hanging from nearly every branch. If I hadn't seen a cat to chase in a few days, I could always count on spotting several squirrels here, burying their nuts. When they saw me, they sprinted in every direction, leaping to the tree, house, and fence. Chasing them was the highlight of the day. I never caught one, though. Not exactly sure what I would have done if I did. Afterwards, I'd lie in a shallow hole in the soft dirt under the boy's window.

"Is that you, Surf?" The window opened and out popped the boy's head. He looked down at me. "I heard you breathing."

One particular squirrel twitched its fluffed-up tail and chirped in anger.

"Always the instigator, aren't you?" the boy said, shaking his head. "If Mama ever saw you bothering her squirrels, she'd get a broom after you."

A broken screen leaned against the house beneath the window. The boy had shoved it out a few weeks ago when I first met him. He placed half a sandwich on the windowsill. I wasted no time standing up with my front paws on the windowsill and scarfing down the sandwich.

"You normally come by on the weekend. I wasn't expecting you today or I'd have more for you. Tell you what, I'll get you a treat and meet you out front."

When he came out onto the front porch, he was in a chair with wheels. Both his legs were wrapped in white stuff and he never moved them. He threw me a couple potato chips and took a bite of his half of the sandwich. "I've been following you on social media. I even had my girlfriend draw your picture on my casts. You're more popular than our quarterback."

I sniffed the ground for any crumbs.

"Melanie will be over later," the boy continued. "She's helping me with my homework. If you stay long enough you might get to visit with her, too."

He shifted in his chair and I tried to nip at a fly buzzing in my left ear. "Thanks for checking on me. I still can't believe that two days after I break my legs, you show up, chasing squirrels, and sleeping under my window. It's as if someone sent you to me. You're like my hero, Surf Dude. I read about all the places you travel and the people who see you. In your own weird way, you're my new best friend. Well, except for Melanie!"

He threw a few more potato chips at me and I caught them before they hit the ground. I looked at him for a moment, wagged my tail, and walked back to the oak tree. Three squirrels had ventured down to the ground, but quickly ran back up.

"See you soon, Surf Dude," he called and went back inside.

Chapter Sixteen

I'd discovered a culvert near the campground the other day, when I chased a squirrel. It was the perfect place to lie down and stay cool on hot days, while I watched and waited for Russ. I had a perfect view to see both ways down Surf Road. Sometimes, I crawled to the back of the culvert and took a nap, away from the eyes of walkers and other dogs.

I'd left the house early one morning, before the sun came up, and dozed in the culvert while I waited for Russ to arrive. Something kicked up the dirt just outside of the culvert, waking me up. An oversized cat crouched in the grass in front of the opening of the culvert. I'd never seen a cat this big. My instinct was to chase it, but those unblinking, pale yellow eyes told me that wouldn't be a good idea. Now I knew what the squirrels felt like when they were hunted.

The cat's short fur was a little darker than mine. Its long tail flicked to the left, then the right. The cat stretched its head to the entrance of the culvert and its pupils dilated into round black orbs, outlined with a sliver of yellow. I braced my back legs and growled. The cat laid its ears back flat against its head.

I'd been scratched on the nose by a cat before, and it hurt almost as bad as those palmetto bushes I fell into when I was running from the gator. The claws on this cat would slice my face to pieces, let alone what those teeth would do to me. Nope, I'd just shuffle a little farther back into the culvert. I hoped it was too small for the cat to crawl inside. There's a reason I'd lived this long on my own; I didn't do stupid things and I avoided confrontations.

I inched back a bit, trying to look smaller and less appetizing. The cat reached a paw into the culvert opening, judging the distance and deciding if it could squeeze in. I would have stayed there all day if I hadn't heard children laughing and running around.

A little girl ran over to the edge of the campground, near my culvert. "A kitty! I see a kitty." I recognized her voice. It was Rosey, a little girl who always threw me peanut butter crackers when her mom and dad weren't looking. Her giggles made me want to play with her, almost.

The cat turned its attention toward Rosey. Its neck muscles flexed. Its body shifted in her direction. It flattened its body in the tall grass near the culvert. This cat had a mild curiosity with me, but the little girl had its complete and utter attention. Her shoes crunched louder in the grass as she came closer.

Not my Rosey! I charged out of the culvert and latched onto the cat's throat. We rolled into the road in front of an oncoming car. Wheels screeched. Rosey screamed and tossed her peanut butter crackers in the air. The cat kicked me loose with its back legs. In two leaps, it crossed the road and disappeared into the woods. I ran after it to make sure it was good and gone. I covered an area of at least five acres, but I never found the cat.

Satisfied that the cat wouldn't bother Rosey, I went back to the feeding place. Russ was already there.

"I've been calling and calling," he said. "It's about time you showed up. You know it's not always about you, Dude."

If only you knew what I've been through this morning, Russ.

He filled my water bowl with cold water and I drank in big gulps.

"I brought fresh chicken that I made. I came by last night with it, but there was only a buzzard here waiting on me."

Russ looked at me for a response, but I ignored him and kept on drinking.

"I ain't leaving food for buzzards. They get enough to eat from the side of the road, so I took it back home."

Russ dropped the chicken meat in the bowl, but I smelled something else besides chicken. His clothes smelled like dog and it wasn't me. I stretched my neck, sniffing his shoes and the back of his pants legs, then trotted over to his Jeep and whiffed a tire. Yep, another dog had been there. I peed on the tire.

"Ah, you smell Skippy, don't you? Don't worry, we're just taking care of my daughter's dog while she's out of town. I haven't replaced you… yet."

I ate the rest of the chicken and left.

I was trotting along the side of the road when a black truck came up behind me. "Hey, Surf Dude!" A teenage boy hung out the passenger window, waved, and whistled at me. The driver honked twice and kept driving.

Later, someone threw chicken nuggets at me out their car window. "Enjoy the chicken, Surf Dude."

I sniffed the nuggets and left them on the side of the road. It wouldn't be there long; a buzzard had followed me for the past mile, waiting to eat all the scraps people tossed. I guess the buzzards knew, wherever I was, there was sure to be food. When you're famous, everyone follows you.

◊◊◊

Russ brought beef stew with rice the next morning. I ate it all and wanted more. Fighting off big cats builds up an appetite.

"I heard you saved Rosey," Russ said as he sat on the bench. "Is there nothing you can't do?"

I didn't stay to chat with Russ. He looked disappointed when I took off, but I'm sure he knew I'd be back later. I always came back.

A new neighborhood was being built not too far from the feeding place. Today was a great day to check it out. I passed orange cones on a partially paved road and houses with men on their roofs, banging away with hammers. One man filled his yellow hat with water for me. Two of the men sat on the tailgate of their truck, tossing me parts of their sandwiches. One put something in a bowl that he called potato salad. It tasted gross and made me gag. I left it there for the ants.

Two houses down, a girl walked outside of her house and into her back yard. She carried a phone like Russ's, only pink, and a bag of chips. "Mom, I'm going to lie in the hammock for a while."

The hammock cast a perfect spot of shade, and with my full tummy, it was a fine place to take a snooze. Preoccupied with her phone, the girl didn't notice that I'd curled up in a ball beneath her. I listened while she talked on her phone.

"Hey Kimmy, I'm on Surf's social media page. This dog is so cool. He goes everywhere. I swear if he could walk to Alaska, he probably would."

Two broken chips fell through the hammock's webbing and I ate them.

"We've been here about a month and I haven't seen him yet, but I hope to."

I nudged a sharp pebble from beneath my chin and rested on the soft grass, waiting for more chips.

"You saw him? Oh, I'm so jealous!" She shifted in the hammock. "I want to go down to the feeding place to see him, but Mama doesn't want to be bothered with it." She hung her left foot over the hammock, bare toes just inches from my face. I sniffed them, crinkled my nose, and almost sneezed. "She doesn't understand what it's like to be a teenager and trapped at home. I can't wait to get a car. I can travel like Surf Dude and go anywhere I want." She giggled. "Is that your mom calling you? Okay, later."

The girl hung her hand over the side of the hammock, still holding her phone. Her fingers smelled like barbeque chips. A few minutes passed and she snored lightly. We both took naps, until her mother called her.

"Octavia, supper is ready!"

Supper! Russ was probably waiting on me. I stood up, stretched, and darted away.

The girl sat up tall in the hammock, staring at me. "What? Are you kidding me? Surf?"

I turned at the sound of my name. I wagged my tail and picked up speed, turning the corner of her house, and was gone in a flash.

◊◊◊

This time, Russ made me wait. I had almost given up on him when he zoomed into the feeding place.

"Whew, I made it. I wasn't sure if you'd wait or not. I got a call that you were here." He filled my bowl with shrimp and hushpuppies. I ate a few and spat out the last one. It tasted funny.

95

"Dang it, Dude. That's expensive medicine there." Russ picked up the soggy hushpuppy. He grumbled and pulled out a doughnut.

I whimpered. *Speed it up, Russ.*

"Be patient. As old Abe Lincoln would say, 'Good things come to those who wait'."

It had been a long time since I had eaten a regular doughnut. I ate it whole. I didn't taste the dry powdery stuff until it slid down my throat, too late to spit it out. I hawked at his feet.

"It serves you right for not eating the hushpuppy," Russ scolded. "Sorry to ruin dessert, but next time, eat the dang hushpuppy."

Chapter Seventeen

People discard unwanted items on the side of the road all the time. I'd found good things and strange things. One morning, I noticed a cardboard box in the grass about half a mile from the feeding place. I didn't think much about it and kept walking.

As I got closer, the box moved and something inside yelped. In the words of Russ, 'Good things come to those who wait,' but I was pretty sure nothing good was going to come out of that box, and I didn't want to wait around to find out.

I walked past the box with no intention of stopping, but it moved again and fell sideways. The top flap pushed up and out jumped a puppy. He leaped from the box, raced in my direction, and ran circles around me.

Usually, I smelled fear from small animals that came close, but not this one. He attached himself to me like a tick. His long white hair hung in his face and was matted around his ears. The rest was tangled with small twigs and leaves. A few of Russ's meals would do him good.

I'd had enough of his yipping and prancing around and tried to slip away, but he followed, nipping at my heels. He almost stepped out in front of a car, and would have if I hadn't bitten his tail and pulled him away from the road.

He followed me on the way to meet Russ. I usually took a nap at the edge of the woods when waiting on Russ, but that puppy had different ideas. He nipped me repeatedly, growling

97

fiercely as if I wasn't four times his size. Nope, I wasn't going to get a nap with that business going on. Yellow flies were less annoying than him. He finally fell asleep with his face buried in my fur.

Russ arrived and I stood up. The puppy didn't move. I encouraged him to follow, but he didn't budge. I left him and went to Russ.

"Hey, Dude! Are you hungry? I brought all kinds of food. Let's see here: steak, chicken, pork, coleslaw, hushpuppies, minus the meds, and…well, I'm not too sure what that is, but I'll bet it's good." Russ cleaned my bowls and filled them with food and water. The puppy remained at the edge of the woods and I whined for him to come.

"What is it, Dude? Eat up."

I picked up a hushpuppy and ran to the woods, dropped it at the pup's feet, and ran back to Russ.

"What are you doing? Stay put and eat before the ants get it." Russ sat down on the bench and read his newspaper. I grabbed a chunk of steak and dashed back to the pup, who was awake now. I dropped the meat where the hushpuppy had been. The pup wagged his tail and devoured it. I ran back to Russ again.

"You got a girlfriend in there?" he asked when I returned. "I don't see her."

I carried a couple pieces of steak a few feet away, buried them for later, and nibbled some more.

"Do you want to hear the latest from your never-ending fandom?" Russ looked at his phone. "Instead of you traveling to other counties and people getting excited about catching a glimpse of you, people are now traveling *here*, hoping to see you. I'm not just talking about traveling from the next county either. I'm talking about the next state!"

An ant crawled between my toes and bit me. I stomped my foot and chewed, trying to get the ant off of me.

"Stop messing around and pay attention. This domed doghouse is like a landmark in Panacea now. People are posting pictures of themselves standing beside it."

I chewed harder, focusing on the itch.

"How you got so popular is beyond me. I'm just waiting for someone to post a picture of a newborn baby on your social media page and name it after you." Russ shook his head.

◊◊◊

I never was able to get the puppy to come out and visit Russ. He was scared of people, just like I was when I first came down here. He slept at the house with me and almost caught Marvin, but Marvin was too fast and there were a million crevices for a mouse to hide in. After a few days, the puppy bored of chasing him.

Anytime I visited with Russ, the pup stayed out of sight. That is until one day when Rosey came back to the campground.

Rosey's hands were full of peanut butter crackers. She sat in the grass a few feet away and tossed crackers to the puppy until he practically crawled in her lap trying to steal them from her mouth. It was embarrassing.

I liked Rosey, but I never got that close. The puppy didn't even resist when she tucked him under her arm and carried him back to her camper. His tail wagged the entire way. A few days later, she walked him on a small leash. He pranced along beside her, eating peanut butter crackers, and rolling over for belly rubs. She'd cleaned him, brushed him, and pulled his hair back out of his eyes with a red ribbon. She called him Coconut.

Who names a dog Coconut? I know my name used to be Honeybun, but at least honey buns taste good. Coconut was disgusting. Poor puppy, he just didn't understand what being a dog meant: freedom, eat when you want, sleep when you want, and never having to wear ribbons in your hair. By the following Saturday, Rosey and Coconut were gone from the campground.

I sorta missed the puppy, but Rosey camped here three times a year. I was sure I'd see them both again.

I'd always been a dog that liked my routine. So the day I went to meet Russ and discovered my doghouse, bowls, bench, and Russ were gone, I wasn't happy. I waited for him for a change instead of him waiting for me. A guy rode by on his bike and waved. Two joggers stopped in front of me, pointed their phones at me, and jogged on.

I'd never waited this long for anything. Russ better have some good food to make up for this. I knew I was in the right place. A faint, familiar sound caught my ear. That was Russ's voice! I found him about half a mile down the road.

"I've been calling you, Dude. Aren't dogs supposed to have great hearing?" He ate a piece of a honey bun.

I didn't like this place. It was on an old dirt road, tucked away from the campground, and it smelled like cats. "I'm going to feed you here for a while. People keep leaving you food in your bowl. We're out of sight here, and this way, you'll be hungry and take your heartworm, flea, and tick meds." Russ spooned a chicken pot pie into the bowl. "It's a little off the beaten path, but that's a good thing."

He settled down on a chair with his newspaper. I stared at him, disgruntled.

"Go ahead, eat up." Russ lowered the papers, "Aren't you going to eat?"

I sat down and turned my head away from the food.

"It's chicken pot pie. I made it myself," he coaxed.

I wanted the old place back; I could see who was coming and going in plenty of time to get out of their way and not be seen. If we stayed here, I wouldn't see anyone until they were practically behind me. Not only that, but this new place smelled like cat-pee. Nope, I didn't like this one bit. I closed my eyes in protest.

"Hmm. Well, I'll try again tomorrow. Good night, Dude." Russ picked up the leftovers, tossed them far back in the wooded area, and cleaned the bowl.

I watched until he was out of sight, then walked over to the woods and ate what he had tossed out. I was irritated, but I wasn't stupid.

Russ tried again for the next few days in the same place, but I didn't eat. I hid behind some bushes and watched him. He walked to the highway and searched for me in all directions. He threw his hat in the dirt, fussed, picked his hat back up, and climbed in his Jeep. He waited on a couple cars to pass before pulling out onto the highway.

I walked right in front of the Jeep, with my tail held high, and marched over to my bowl.

Russ sat in the Jeep for a minute, backed up, and parked beside the dog house.

"Where you been? I've been here an hour." He tossed my food carelessly in the bowl, spilling it. I sniffed it and gave Russ the stink-eye. It was dog food! He'd mixed it with the good stuff again. I pulled out a few chunks of chicken and ate them. The rest stayed in the bowl and a few flies swarmed it while I drank water from another bowl.

"Change isn't always a bad thing, Dude. You'll get used to this new spot."

I didn't stay to visit and headed home.

"Hey, where are you going, Dude?"

I paused long enough to woof at him and kept walking in the same direction.

"Fine, I'll find another stray dog to give this too! Better yet, a cat!"

Chapter Eighteen

Russ had told me a few times that he liked to go to church on Sundays. Since my boycott of the new feeding spot, I missed seeing Russ something awful, but I knew I'd see him at the church.

Tables were set out on the lawn, piled high with food. It smelled like everything Russ had ever fed me. I wanted to see Russ, but first I planned to see what was in that large steaming bowl, over on the left corner of a fold-out table.

While the men were preoccupied moving an ice chest around and the ladies focused on the children playing volleyball, I casually strolled to the table and hid under the long, crocheted tablecloth. I knew every dish they brought to the table by the way it smelled. I should have taken what was in that steaming bowl and left, but....

I stuck my head out from under the table, within inches of the bowl, when a little freckle-faced boy with curly crimson hair spotted me.

"It's Surf Dude!" His piercing voice drew the attention of everyone.

When crazy-eyed children chase after you, it's more frightening than the group of deer jumping over my head. I ran the length of the table, and tangled my toenail in the tablecloth yarn at the opposite end. It trailed behind me as I ran down the bike trail with half the food still on it. Women, men, and children chased me. No food was worth all that drama.

I dodged between bushes and shucked off the tablecloth. I was free, but I left a trail of food, and a bunch of angry people, in my wake. I never did get to see what was in that steaming bowl.

◊◊◊

For the next few days, I ate with Tully at his camper in the woods. He'd forgiven me for the mess I made.

"Dude, I'm about to swear off women and become a hermit." Tully took a bite of his hotdog. "Gracie-Lou's done lost her mind if she thinks I'm moving to New York. Too crowded, too busy, and too full of strangers. I'm a country boy. Give me a grill, a few beers, a creek to fish in, woods to hunt, with a yellow dog, and I'm a happy man."

Tully dropped a spoonful of baked beans on a paper plate and put it on the floor. "You got a girlfriend, Dude? If you do, bring her around sometime; I'd like to meet her."

I ate the beans, but wondered what Russ might have for me.

◊◊◊

When a dog doesn't have a purpose, it causes problems. We get bored and get in trouble. I'm *not* an exception to that rule. My dog instinct made me chase anything that ran or was thrown. It was a pretty sure thing that if you threw a ball, I would chase it, but you might not get it back.

I've discovered a game called "golf." People walk around carrying sticks, ride small cars on the grass, and swing at small white balls. After breakfast with Tully one day, I wandered down to the golf course and watched as a man played golf. He yelled and swung his stick. The white ball sailed through the air, hit the ground, and rolled to my feet. I stared at it, sniffed it, and tried to bite it. It was hard as a rock. I spat it back out.

"Hey, get away from that!" the man yelled. He marched over to me, waving his stick in the air. I backed up and watched him reach for the ball.

"No!" another guy yelled. "You have to play the ball where it lands, Ben. You know that."

The first man swung hard with the stick, missed the ball, and yelled at both the stick and the ball. Strangest thing I'd ever seen. He swung again, missed, and flung the stick across the open field. I don't know what got into me, but I ran in, scooped the ball in my mouth, and took off across the field.

The man ran behind me, ranting, but I dodged through the pines of the nearby woods and hid the ball in a culvert. If I could have rescued the stick too, I would have, but the ball had to do.

◊◊◊

One afternoon, I raced down Surf Road trying to outrun a yellow fly when I saw Russ's Jeep parked in the old feeding place. I bolted down the sidewalk, jumped, barked, and even spun in circles. In my excitement, I almost jumped in the back of his Jeep.

"You know, I was just joking about giving your food to a cat, right?" Russ stirred my food and placed the bowl at my feet. "Rumor around Panacea is that you invited yourself to lunch on the church grounds. You're a mess, you know that, Dude? When people change things on me, I get outta sorts too. We'll just keep meeting here if that's good with you."

He poured water in another bowl. I ate and drank everything. I laid beside the food bowl, resting my mouth on the rim, and stared at him as he pulled out his phone.

"There's talk of painting the water tower here and putting something on it about you. I can see it now. 'Panacea, Florida, Home of Surf Dog.'" Russ looked up at the water tower. "Has a nice ring to it. You gotta be someone special to get your name up there."

Russ pulled out a honey bun and broke off a piece. I didn't even care when it bounced off my nose and hit the ground. I ate it, dirt and all.

"A friend of mine sent me an article about dogs and what breed everyone thinks you are." Russ pulled papers from his Jeep and sat on the bench. "Apparently, your breed has a lot of names: American Dingo, Common Indian Dog, Dixie Dog, Primitive Dog, and my favorite, Carolina Dog."

I tilted my head, watching Russ read the paper.

"Hmm, are you a New Guinea Singing Dog?"

I whimpered.

"I didn't think so. They're speculating that your ancestors came over here with primitive peoples when they crossed the Bering Strait. The person who wrote the article believes that your breed hasn't changed much, and you still look pretty much like you did 14,000 years ago."

Russ looked at me and then looked at the papers again. "Dang, Dude, that's pretty cool. A lot of your kin settled in Georgia and South Carolina in isolated areas without being domesticated by people. Huh, that explains a lot." He flipped the page. "Hey, listen to this."

My ears perked up.

"Most experts say that you don't take too kindly to strangers and don't trust people. Ha! That sounds like a few people I know, as well as a certain spoiled dog." He grinned. "They describe what you look like too. Stand up, Dude, let me see if they're right."

I yawned, stretched my front paws out, and rolled over in the sand onto my back to get an itch that had been bothering me all afternoon.

"If you ain't a full breed Carolina Dog, you're pretty dang close."

He read a bit more and frowned. "It says here that you're a pack-dog and like to be with other dogs." Russ lowered his glasses and squinted at me over the rims. "Hmm, I guess they can't be right on everything."

I stretched out on the warm sand, yawned again, and closed my eyes.

"I'm glad we moved back here, too," Russ said.

I turned over to look at him and crossed my front paws, one over the other.

Russ pointed his phone at me. "Ah, that's a great picture. You have me wrapped around your little toe."

Yes, sir, I sure do, I thought.

"It looks like our relationship is a lot of give and take. I give you food and you take it or leave it." Russ stretched an arm across the back of the bench.

No relationship is perfect, Russ.

"Dude, I've been feeding you here for about three years now. Sometimes I wonder how you even survive with all the hurricanes, yellow flies, mosquitoes, wild animals, and crazy drivers. But you always seem to come out on top. You're like the eighth wonder of the world. It wouldn't surprise me when they build another high school in this county, if they want you as the mascot. People are making shirts, mugs, and key chains with your face on them. They love you that much."

I finished rolling, stood up, and shook.

"I don't think you realize how much you mean to people," Russ continued. "This is a crazy world we live in. People are dealing with stress every day: finances, health, death, divorces. I guess reading about you and your courage and survival, gives people strength and hope. You bring them a little bit of happiness."

Russ leaned over, bracing his elbows on his knees. "Let me tell you something, man to man. I wouldn't do this for just anyone. I'm hoping one day that you'll trust me enough to come home with me. You'd get all the chicken and dumplings, shrimp, and hushpuppies your little doggie heart desires. I know the hushpuppy-dealer personally." Russ winked.

He just said the magic word, hushpuppy, but I didn't smell any.

"I'll even stop trying to get you to eat dog food. There's a nice couch to sleep on and a warm fireplace for cold nights. Whatcha say there, Dude, how about today?"

I walked to Russ, and sniffed his hand. He twitched his pinky finger and I licked the sugar off it.

"You've never done that before." Russ smiled. "I guess there's hope for us."

I looked at the Jeep and back at Russ.

One day, Russ. Maybe one day….

Acknowledgements

It all began when a small group of people started caring for a stray dog in Panacea, Florida. This is no ordinary dog, mind you. This dog has evaded capture, hurricanes, crazy drivers, and wild animals. His popularity grew among the community, prompting the creation of a Facebook page titled *The Adventures of Bill & SurfDude*. Surf Dude, as he came to be known, has fans throughout the United States and abroad, too. I became a follower of Surf Dude's expeditions a little over a year ago.

To Rhett DeVane, a fellow author and friend, whose gentle nudge, actually a push, convinced me to contact Bill Russell, one of a few dedicated caregivers of Surf Dude. Without Rhett's call that afternoon, and her proofreading skills of my raw words on paper, I'm not sure if this novel would ever have been written.

To Bill Russell, I knew it was hit or miss to actually see the dog on my first visit with you, but it was my lucky day, and Surf Dude not only dropped by, but sniffed my fingers and posed for several pictures. As you suggested, I respected Surf Dude's boundaries and didn't attempt to touch him; I was rewarded with a long visit and an opportunity to chat with you about Surf Dude's history.

To M.R. Street, my publisher at Turtle Cove Press, a follower of Surf Dude and friend, I can't think of anyone who is more excited than me about the fruition of this novel coming to print.

About the Author

Zelle Andrews was born and raised in Tallahassee, Florida. With an interest in writing since she was twelve, she still has her first diary, which was given to her as a Christmas present by her parents. Married since 1987, Zelle has infused tidbits of her life with her husband and two children in her first two published novels, *Paisley Memories* and *Dancing with Dandelions*. *The Adventures of Surf Dude: The Dog of Ochlockonee Bay* is her third published novel. Book Three in the Paisley series is forthcoming. Zelle is currently writing a historical novel, tentatively titled *Mercy Jane,* about the Salem witch trials. Zelle is a member of the Florida Authors and Publishers Association as well as the Tallahassee Writers Association.

About the Real Surf Dude
Ambassador for Homeless Dogs

Surf Dude is a senior dog who has been travelling the roads, running away from storms and fireworks, for many years. He is believed to be a Carolina Dog, but no one knows his true origin and why he came to the Florida coast. This gave me the freedom to use my imagination and create his beginning.

Surf recently decided to give up the vagabond life and retire to a home where he is loved and cared for. His long-time caregivers ask that, to honor Surf Dude, you help homeless dogs by volunteering at a shelter, contributing funds or needed items to a rescue group, or foster or adopt your next furry family member from a rescue or shelter.

Other Books by Zelle Andrews

Paisley Memories: The Beginning of Me*

Dancing with Dandelions: The Beginning of Us*

Other Books from Turtle Cove Press

Blue Rock Rescue, by M.R. Street*

Dahlia in Bloom, by Susan Koehler*

From Salvation to Salve: My Journey to Happiness,
by Suzan E. Zan*

The Health Is Power League in Attack of Zombacon,
by M.R. Street*

The Hunter's Moon, by M.R. Street

Nobody Kills Uncle Buster and Gets Away with It,
by Susan Koehler

Snowden's Story: One Marine's Indebtedness to the Corps,
by Lt. Gen. Lawrence F. Snowden, USMC (Ret.)*

The Werewolf's Daughter, by M.R. Street*

*Award winners

turtle cove press

https://www.turtlecovepress.com

CPSIA information can be obtained
at www.ICGtesting.com
Printed in the USA
LVHW041133041221
705203LV00015B/1773